T0277323

WHERE
THERE'S
SMOKE

OTHER BOOKS BY KIKI SWINSON

PLAYING DIRTY
NOTORIOUS
WIFEY
I'M STILL WIFEY
LIFE AFTER WIFEY
THE CANDY SHOP
A STICKY SITUATION
STILL WIFEY MATERIAL
STILL CANDY SHOPPING
WIFE EXTRAORDINAIRE
WIFE EXTRAORDINAIRE RETURNS
CHEAPER TO KEEP HER
CHEAPER TO KEEP HER 2
THE SCORE
CHEAPER TO KEEP HER 3
CHEAPER TO KEEP HER 4
THE MARK
CHEAPER TO KEEP HER 5
DEAD ON ARRIVAL
THE BLACK MARKET
THE SAFE HOUSE, BLACK MARKET 2
PROPERTY OF THE STATE, BLACK MARKET 3
THE DEADLINE
PUBLIC ENEMY # 1
PLAYING WITH FIRE
BURNING SEASON
WHERE THERE'S SMOKE

WHERE THERE'S SMOKE

KIKI SWINSON

www.kensingtonbooks.com

This book is a work of fiction. Names, characters, businesses, organizations, places, events, and incidents either are the product of the author's imagination or are used fictitiously. Any resemblance to actual persons, living or dead, events, or locales is entirely coincidental.

To the extent that the image or images on the cover of this book depict a person or persons, such person or persons are merely models, and are not intended to portray any character or characters featured in the book.

DAFINA BOOKS are published by

Kensington Publishing Corp.
900 Third Avenue
New York, NY 10022

Copyright © 2024 by Kiki Swinson

All rights reserved. No part of this book may be reproduced in any form or by any means without the prior written consent of the Publisher, excepting brief quotes used in reviews.

All Kensington Titles, Imprints, and Distributed Lines are available at special quantity discounts for bulk purchases for sales promotions, premiums, fund-raising, and educational or institutional use. Special book excerpts or customized printings can also be created to fit specific needs. For details, write or phone the office of the Kensington special sales manager: Kensington Publishing Corp., 900 Third Avenue, New York, NY 10022, attn: Special Sales Department, Phone: 1-800-221-2647.

The DAFINA logo is a trademark of Kensington Publishing Corp.

Library of Congress Control Number: 2023951504

ISBN: 978-1-4967-3902-5
First Kensington Hardcover Edition: May 2024

ISBN-13: 978-1-4967-3904-9 (ebook)

10 9 8 7 6 5 4 3 2 1

Printed in the United States of America

WHERE THERE'S SMOKE

CHAPTER 1

Alayna

*P*RICILLA SAT THERE PATIENTLY AND WAITED FOR ME TO SAY SOME-thing as my legs rocked back and forth, the palms of my hands sweaty. I was clearly not in the right headspace to give her the complete rundown of what had just happened. It was too much, so I immediately began constructing lies in my head. I had become so good at it now that it took me no time to think of what I'd tell Pricilla.

After two full minutes of complete silence, she urged me to speak. "Can you tell me what's really going on?" She broke my train of thought.

"Girl, it just all happened so fast. I was standing there talking to Tim, and then out of nowhere, two guys came from behind his car with guns in hand, demanded that he give them his money. When Tim resisted, they shot him and took his wallet anyway. I was telling him to give it to them, but he wouldn't listen. And now he's gone."

I tried to sound as heartbroken as possible. I even let out a couple of crocodile tears. I couldn't let on that I was behind this murder and that her brother, K-Rock, and his friend Russell were the gunmen. I couldn't trust her with that type of information, regardless of the fact this hit was done to bring my brother home. Because knowing the truth could actually alter a person's mind.

"Why are you crying?" she asked with a puzzled look on her face.

"Because I saw a man get killed right in front of my face," I explained, my voice rising and falling with emotion.

Pricilla's facial expression was unsympathetic. "But he was a traitor. He was going to testify against your brother."

"I know," I said, and then I let out a loud sigh. "But I still loved the guy."

"He broke your heart, for God's sake."

"So I'm supposed to be happy that he's dead?" I asked her. Around this time guilt was starting to set in.

"As far as I'm concerned, he got what he deserved," Pricilla said with finality. She made it perfectly clear that she had no sympathy for him.

I, on the other hand, was starting to feel different. I swear, I can't say where this was coming from. "Look, can we have some respect for the dead?" I lamented. Pricilla was starting to get underneath my skin, even though I knew she meant well.

"Fuck him! Let his wife and family pay their respects. We've got other things to do, like get your brother out of jail."

"Whatcha think I've been doing?" I became more annoyed.

"Look, we're getting off focus. Are you staying here tonight or are you going home?" she asked.

"I'm staying here."

"Well, let's drop this whole conversation and get some rest. We need to save all of our energy for your brother. Not for that traitor!"

I let out a long sigh. It was evident that Pricilla was not going to show any compassion for Tim's death. It was a moot issue for her, so I left well enough alone and found a comfy spot on her oversize sofa. After Pricilla handed me a blanket, I crawled into a fetal position and just lay there. I immediately thought about what K-Rock and Russell were doing at this particular moment. Not only had I paid them five grand to murder Tim, I also paid five grand for someone else's head. Eliminating everyone who could testify against my brother and put him away for life had become a top priority of mine.

The plan was to get rid of Tim first, and that other person sometime later, so that the detectives wouldn't immediately connect the two. Now K-Rock didn't say when the next murder would take place, but that it would get done and I would get my report from the news, since it wouldn't be wise to contact each other after tonight. It was better this way when the cops started to look at everyone I interacted with.

During murder investigations detectives always wiretap devices on all murder suspects. It helps them listen in on conversations that may have something to do with the murder that they're investigating. Nine times out of ten, someone always says something to incriminate themselves over the phone. So, to prevent that from happening in this case, we'd already decided that all forms of communication were out of the question. And that they could never speak of this ever again. I can only hope that they keep up their end of the deal because I'm solid over here.

With everything on my mind, I found it very hard to go to sleep. I found myself tossing and turning for most of the night. I couldn't get a wink of sleep. All I did was replay every single detail of Tim's murder. And to see the horror on his face when the guys fired their guns at him was indescribable. He knew he was about to die, so I wondered what he could've been thinking. I mean, could he have known that I'd set him up? If he didn't, I'm sure he knew it by now. Especially since in this afterlife stuff, everybody tended to believe that dead people walked around freely. Well, if that's the case, then he definitely knew that I had his ass killed. And if he knew, then I also hoped he knew that I did it for my brother. It was all about Alonzo's freedom and not because Tim cheated on me with Jesse. My brother became my main priority when I found out that Tim had talked to the cops and turned his back on us. He needed to know that he made it this way. Not us. Too bad, the female special agent wasn't gonna see it this way. In fact, she was going to come for my jugular when she found out that Tim was dead. She was going to hound me until she found a way to lock me up. But I refused to allow that bitch to get one step ahead of me. I knew she was going to be relentless, but I was gonna stay on my toes and show her that she ain't locking nobody up over here. Not while I was still alive. From this day forward I vowed to eliminate anyone who tried to come between me and my brother's freedom. He and I would die first before we would spend the rest of our lives in jail.

CHAPTER 2

Kirsten

*K*NOCK! KNOCK! KNOCK!

Startled by the knocks at the front door, I sat up in my bed and looked at the clock on the nightstand and realized it was a little after midnight, so I got up and walked tentatively toward the front door to see who it was. As I approached, more knocks came.

"Who is it?" I asked as I neared the door.

"Detective Showers and Detective Pittman, ma'am," I heard one man announce.

Curious as to why these guys were here, I opened my door and stood before them, wanting to know what they wanted at this late hour. My porch light was on, and it was shining bright, so I could see the white men dressed in plain clothes, displaying their badges in full view for my benefit. After I acknowledged their presence, I gave them my full attention and looked at them head-on.

"What are your names again?"

"I'm Detective Showers from the homicide division of the Chesapeake Police Department," replied the taller white gentleman.

"And I'm Detective Pittman," said the shorter white man.

"Well, gentlemen, what brings you by?" I got straight to the point.

"Can we come in?" Detective Showers asked.

"Can you tell me what this is about?"

"It's about your husband, ma'am," Detective Showers continued.

"What about my husband?" I asked, instantly becoming alarmed.

"Please let us come inside, ma'am," he insisted.

I hesitated, prolonging their entry, because I wanted my questions answered *now*. "Wait, is he all right?"

"Ma'am, please," Detective Pittman chimed in.

After falling under heavy pressure by the detectives, I decided to let them into my home. "Come on in," I finally agreed.

Both men entered my home and stood in the middle of the floor. They both surveyed the immediate area of our surroundings with one look around.

"Is anyone else here with you?" Detective Pittman wondered aloud.

"Yes, my two children are here. But they're in bed. Why?" I asked as I stood before them.

"We just wanted to be aware of who was in the home," Detective Showers spoke up.

"Can we sit down?" Detective Pittman wanted to know.

"Yes, sure," I told them, and then we all sat down, on either the sofa or love seat. "Now can one of you tell me what this is pertaining to my husband?"

Detective Showers scooted to the edge of the sofa, cleared his throat, and said, "Mrs. Stancil, I'm here to inform you that your husband has been murdered."

Instantly panic-stricken at the idea that my husband was murdered, I clutched the collar of my robe in disbelief. "No, there must be some mistake."

"No, ma'am, I'm afraid there isn't. We found him shot and killed in a salvage junkyard, about fifteen miles from here."

"Wait, but that can't be. I just saw him a few hours ago. He was fine when he left this house." I began to sob, sending bat-size butterflies into my stomach.

"Can you tell me what time that was?" Detective Showers asked.

"It was about a little after nine o'clock. I remember when he came into the house, because I was watching television. And when I saw him, I told him that he was going to live a long time, because I was just talking about him. So he laughed, went to the bathroom, and a few minutes later, he came out. We said a few more words to each other and then he left," I explained.

"What did he say? Did he tell you where he was going? Or who he was meeting?" Detective Showers inquired after taking out a notepad and pen. He waited for me to answer his question so that he could jot down my answer.

"No, he didn't. I assumed he went back to work," I told him.

"Does your husband have any enemies, Mrs. Stancil?"

"Not to my knowledge. Everyone loved him."

"Does he owe anyone money? Or have any gambling debts?"

"No. My husband didn't gamble." I didn't hesitate to reply to their questions.

"Can you tell us if he was involved in the murder investigation launched by Virginia Beach homicide detectives and the federal agents?" Detective Pittman interjected.

Appalled by his question, I gave him a sharp look and then I bit into my bottom lip. I could feel heat rising up from my chest, and my hands involuntarily curled into fists with intentions of using them at any given moment. "Of course not. Didn't you guys see the news? The man who committed those murders is locked up right now," I said, gritting my teeth. I mean, how dare these men ask me such a question? My husband was an honorable man.

"Listen, Mrs. Stancil, we aren't trying to accuse your husband of any wrongdoing. We're just trying to get to the bottom of why someone wanted to murder him," Detective Pittman chimed back in.

"Why don't you talk to Alayna. It wouldn't surprise me if she was behind my husband's murder," I hissed, looking at both detectives seriously.

"We've talked to her. She was there at the scene when it happened," Detective Showers pointed out.

I hopped up from the sofa and shouted, "I knew it! That fucking bitch had my husband killed, and I'm not going to let her get away with it!"

Detective Showers stood up and waved both hands. "Wait, hold on! We don't know that for sure," he acknowledged.

"You found them both at a junkyard, right?"

"Yes."

"Well, did she tell you why they were there?"

"She acknowledged that they were having an affair . . ." Detective Showers started explaining.

"I freaking knew it. That dirty slut!" I roared, my voice cracking with pain and anger. I was visibly shaken; my eyebrows shot up and my pulse sped up. I could only take so much shit when it came to hearing about my husband and that tramp. A woman's intuition was always spot-on. And here I was standing in my living room with two detectives telling me that Alayna confessed to being my husband's mistress. Fucking bitch!

"Wait, Mrs. Stancil, hold on. Just hear us out," Detective Pittman interjected.

"Yes, and why don't you have a seat? You don't wanna wake up your kids, right?" Detective Showers said calmly.

I instantly reacted, thought for a second, and knew the detectives were right. I didn't want to wake up my kids. They didn't need to hear this about their father. Not like this. So I took the advice of the cops and sat back down on the edge of the sofa. But I stayed on high alert.

Detective Showers sat back down across from me and began to tell me everything Alayna had told them. I eyed the detective evilly, my nostrils moving in and out. I had one shaky finger jutted toward the floor while my other hand was balled so tightly my nails dug moon-shaped craters into my palms. I swear, I was tired of hearing the bullshit-ass story Alayna had given them, and I was two seconds from telling them that. In my assessment there was nothing else for them to say that would convince me that Alayna didn't have anything to do with Tim's murder. In my eyes this was an open-and-shut case. And I made sure I expressed that to the detectives.

"Listen, I don't care what Alayna told you guys. I believe strongly that she either killed my husband or had someone do it. So you need to get out of here and get the evidence you need to put her behind bars for the rest of her life," I barked at them, and then I stood back up on my feet. This was a clear indication that this conversation was over and that I was ready for them to leave.

"Well, we want to thank you for your time," Detective Pittman said, and stood up.

Detective Showers stood up behind him. "Yes, thank you. And just know that we're gonna work hard to find your husband's killers and bring them to justice," he added.

"Please do, because if you don't, I'm gonna go out there and find them myself."

"We don't need you to do anything, Mrs. Stancil. Let us do our jobs," Detective Showers insisted, and then he handed me his business card. "If you hear anything, please give me a call."

I took his card and showed them both to the front door. Heading out, they advised me that the city morgue would contact me about Tim's body, and then they both expressed their condolences. When I closed the door behind them, it felt like a ton of bricks had fallen on top of me and I collapsed onto the floor and began to sob like a baby. I was beginning to feel like I was losing my mind on all fronts, but then I figured that it wouldn't be any good for my children if I let them see me like this. I needed to pull myself together and regroup. If not for me, then for Tim and our children.

CHAPTER 3

Jesse

I CALLED TIM OVER A DOZEN TIMES AND ALL MY CALLS WENT STRAIGHT to voicemail, which, of course, had me worried because this was not like him. I knew something was wrong because he would've either called me back or he would've come back to the station by now. I wanted so badly to go look for him, but I'm under strict orders to stay at the station no matter what. So I went to Paul's room and knocked on his door. Surprisingly, he was up FaceTiming his girlfriend. He opened the door and greeted me, "What's up?" He held his cell phone in his hand.

"Got a minute?" I wanted to know.

He looked down on the screen of his phone and told his girl-friend that he'd call her back in a moment. After she hung up, he let me in his room, and I closed the door behind me. I stood a few feet away from the door because Paul blocked me from moving farther into his room. I couldn't tell you what that was about, but at this point it didn't matter. I was only there to talk about Tim and what I had to say wasn't going to take long.

Paul stood in front of me and folded his arms across his chest. "What's going on?"

"Talk to Tim?" I asked him.

"No. As a matter of fact, I haven't. Why?"

"Because I've been trying to reach him, and I haven't been able to contact him."

"Tried his cell phone?"

"Over a dozen times."

"What about paging him?"

"I tried that too."

"Maybe he's had an emergency at home, and he can't answer."

"No, I think it's something else."

"What do you mean?"

"When he left here, he told me that he was going to go meet Alayna so they could talk. And that was over three hours ago. It's not like him to not report back to the station and not answer his phone."

Paul thought for a second and then said, "Yeah, you're right. Have you tried calling his home?"

"I don't have the number."

"Wait, I have it on my cell phone." Paul started sifting through the contact list in his phone. Meanwhile the doorbell rang at the front entrance of the station's building. Paul and I looked at each other. "Think that could be him?" he wondered.

"Why would he ring the bell when he has a key?" I pointed out.

Before giving Paul a chance to answer, I exited his room and he followed on my heels. My heart raced as I headed toward the front entrance of the station. Paul and I could see the silhouette of two people standing on the other side of the partial wooden and glass engraved door.

"I wonder who that could be, at this time of the morning?" I questioned.

"Beats me," Paul replied as we continued toward the front entrance.

After we reached the door, Paul opened it. Standing on the

outside of the entryway were two white men, who immediately identified themselves as homicide detectives.

"I'm Detective Pittman," the first one said.

"And I'm Detective Showers," the other announced.

They showed Paul and me their badges and asked if they could come in to talk. We let them in and that's when they told us why they were here. They started out asking us questions about Tim, leading us to believe he was in trouble or indicating that he was involved in something serious. Like the first question was, what time did he leave the station? And when he left, did he say where he was going? How was his relationship with his wife? And did he have any enemies? A slew of questions came, one after the next. It became impossible to answer them without constantly asking what this was all about.

"Why all the questions?" I broke down and asked. I felt like it was time to get answers from them.

"Tim is dead," Detective Showers declared.

The news hit me like a ton of bricks. I gasped for air as I held my stomach. My heart instantly started aching. "No, don't tell me that!" I squealed. I regretted that I even let him leave this place. I knew that it was a bad idea. I should've stopped him.

Instantly shocked and confused, Paul asked, "What happened?"

"He was robbed and shot in a salvage junkyard, about twenty miles from here," Detective Showers replied.

"Why was he at a salvage junkyard?" Paul's questions continued.

I couldn't hold back the tears and let the floodgates open as I pictured Tim's lifeless body. This made me angry. "That fucking bitch set him up!" I screeched. My heart started racing overtime.

Paul and both detectives looked at me. "What do you mean, she 'set him up'?" Detective Showers asked.

"Listen, they were having an affair and he ended it," I lied. I knew Alayna ended the relationship, but the cops didn't have to know it.

"So you're saying that she had him killed because he broke off the affair with her?" Detective Pittman asked.

I could tell that he needed clarity. "Yes, that's exactly what I am saying."

"Jesse, those are some pretty strong accusations," Paul pointed out.

"Well, it's the truth," I shot back.

"But you don't know that for sure. I know Alayna and she wouldn't do that to Tim. They were like family."

"You'll do anything in the heat of passion." I wouldn't back down.

"Not Alayna. I know her. She wouldn't harm a fly." Paul stood his ground.

"All right, let's not get carried away. We'll get to the bottom of it, don't you worry," Detective Showers asserted.

"Have you spoken to his wife?" I wanted to know.

"Yes, as a matter of fact, we have," Detective Showers answered, adding, "We just left her residence."

"How did she take the news?" Paul interjected.

"She took it pretty well, actually," Detective Showers continued.

"You don't think she had something to do with it, do you?" Paul questioned the cop.

"It's too soon to say right now."

"How do you know that he was robbed?" Paul continued probing the detective.

"Because that's the story we got from Alayna."

"So she was there?" Paul's reaction changed.

"See, I told you," I grumbled, shaking my head.

"Now hold on, you guys. Just because she was there doesn't mean that she had something to do with it," Detective Pittman chimed in.

"Yes, let's not get ahead of ourselves," Detective Showers added. "We're in the preliminary stages of this investigation. So, once we speak to all parties involved and collect all of our DNA and forensics, we will find out who pulled the trigger and who was involved."

"Well, I hope so, because Tim was a good man and he didn't deserve this," Paul insisted.

"He sure didn't. But I know deep down in my heart that Alayna is behind this whole thing, and I can't wait until you guys take the blinders off and see it for yourself," I retorted as I shot them an evil look.

The detectives knew that I wasn't backing off the idea of Alayna being involved, so they stopped trying to convince me otherwise. They did change the subject and asked if they could search Tim's office. "Gladly," I said first, and led them in the direction of Tim's office. Paul and I left them to go through his things freely and insisted that if they needed us, we'd be in the kitchen area of the station, which was down the opposite end of the hall and directly around the corner.

After we left them alone, Paul and I retreated to the kitchen to talk more. We kept mulling over why would someone want to kill Tim and we couldn't come up with an answer. It was mind-boggling that someone would take his life like that, which brought me back to Alayna's involvement. I knew she had something to do with his murder—so mark my words, it will come out.

"What are we going to do now?" Paul wondered aloud.

"We gotta tell the other guys."

"Let's do it," he said, and then he got up and went looking for the rest of the guys who were in the station.

CHAPTER 4

Alonzo

*L*IKE CLOCKWORK, I GET UP EVERY MORNING AT THE SAME TIME, brush my teeth, and drink a cup of cell-made coffee while I wait for the COs to turn on the phones and TV in the block. When the TV powered up this morning, the channel was programmed from the night before and there was a new broadcast going on when the picture came into full focus. I was sitting in my cell when I saw the story headline at the top of the TV screen of a Virginia Beach fire chief murdered. It threw me for a loop so I got up from my bunk and walked outside my cell to get up close to the action.

"I am standing in front of Chesapeake's Salvage Yard, where the Chesapeake police officers responded to the 2100 block of Dukeland Street around 10:45 p.m. and found a man was shot and killed last night. His name was Tim Stancil, and it is believed that he was robbed before he was murdered, according to one witness. The police have no suspects, but I am told that they are working vigorously to bring the family of this victim some answers. So anyone with information about this case is asked to call the area's Crime Line

at 1-800-LOCK-U-UP. You can also leave an anonymous tip online with Pt3tips. Tipsters won't have to testify in court and could get a cash reward of up to one thousand dollars for information that leads to an arrest. This is Karen Taylor, coming to you live from KGTV."

Stunned by this information, I was both shocked and happy at the same fucking time. I wasted no time in grabbing the nearest phone and getting Pricilla on the line. Thankfully, she answered on the first ring. It almost felt like she was waiting for my call. After she pressed the number 5 button to accept my call, she said, "Hello."

"Hey, baby, what's going on?" I said casually, trying to feel her mood out. See if she knew what was going on before I mentioned it.

"Nothing much. Just sitting here with your sister," she announced. And there you go, that was my cue. They knew something about Tim's murder. Why else would Alayna be there this early in the morning?

"Word? What y'all into early this morning?" I began to probe her.

"Just talking . . ." she said; her answer was flat. I knew Pricilla and she wasn't feeling comfortable in this space where I was trying to put her.

"Talking about what?" I pressed her to see if she could break the ice.

"Wait, I'm going to let her tell you," Pricilla said, and then I heard movement in the background. I knew then that she was handing the phone to Alayna.

"What's up, bro?" she said. But she wasn't that cheerful, like she normally is.

So I said, "What's up with you?" I had to throw the question back at her.

She paused and then she sighed heavily. "Tim's dead," she stated.

"So, what I just saw on the news was true?" I asked, even though I knew that it was a rhetorical question. I think I said it because that was my only follow-up question.

"You saw the news?" she replied gravely.

"Yeah, I just saw it on the news, that's why I called," I added, wanting to seem somewhat concerned. I mean, I was locked up and the phones were being monitored. Even more, now that I was under investigation for three murders. So they were watching me like a hawk.

"I don't want to talk about it too much over this phone, but two guys came from out of nowhere, asked him for his wallet, and when he wouldn't give it to them, they shot him and took it anyway. It all happened so fast," she explained.

"What do you mean, 'it all happened so fast'?"

"I was there, Zo. Tim and I was there talking, and the guys came from out of nowhere."

"Are you all right? Were you hurt?" I asked. She seemed okay, but I wanted to make sure.

"Yes, I'm fine. I'm just shook up a bit. But I'll be fine."

"Do the police know this?"

"Yes, I was the one who called them."

"So y'all were at a salvage junkyard?"

"Yeah, that's where he told me to meet him."

"Think he was followed?"

"I don't know," she said subtly. It was like she had nothing else to say in that area.

"Damn, baby girl, I'm sorry that you had to witness that."

"I just wish that I could've helped him. Maybe then he'd still be alive," she said.

When she said that, I knew she had ordered the hit and that made me smile. She got my message from the Hispanic guy and took matters into her own hands. I fucking loved it. That motherfucker was out of my hair, and all I've gotta do next is get rid of the witness who saw my car parked outside the old dude's house. From there I'm home free.

"Yeah, me too," I said, but knowing deep down in my heart, I was glad that maggot was dead. If I was on the streets, I probably would've killed him myself. Fucking snitch!

"Coming to see me today?" I wanted to know. I needed to see her. Look into her eyes and see if she was really all right. Alayna was a good girl. Not a killer, but she'd do anything for me, so I think it's my duty to check in on her when need be.

"You want me to?" she asked.

"Fuck yeah. I need to see you, especially with everything going on. Damn, I wish that I could hug you. Man, I don't know what I would've done if those motherfuckers would've hurt you. This jail would've definitely had to put me in the hole because I would've lost my fucking mind."

"Well, they didn't, so let's not talk about what-ifs."

"Yeah, you're right. I'm tripping."

"What time you want me to come up there?"

"As soon as you can."

"Want me to bring Pricilla with me?"

"No, I just want to see you. Tell her I'll see her on the next go-round."

"No, you tell her. And I'll see you later."

"A'ight, I love you."

"I love you too," she concluded, and then she handed the phone back to Pricilla.

"Hey, baby, I'm back," Pricilla started up. "How you are feeling?"

"I'm okay, under the circumstances. Can't wait to get out of this motherfucker though."

"So you got something to tell me?" Pricilla got straight to the point.

"Yeah, I told Alayna to come holla at me. But I want you to sit this one out. Is that cool?"

"Yes, I guess it is," she answered, but I could tell she was unsure.

"It's only for this time. I just need to speak with her about some family shit is all."

"I understand," she added. But I knew her, and she didn't like this arrangement one bit. I knew she was struggling with the fact that she wasn't going to be able to see me today. I mean, it's not like she can come see me every day. Visiting days are only twice a week. So the next time she'll be able to see me is in four days.

"You know I'm going to make it up to you when I get out of this joint, right?"

"Yes, of course."

"Have you contacted everyone about pushing the wedding date back?"

"Yes, I have. Everyone knows, including the venue."

"What about the DJ?"

"Yup, I contacted him too and he's on standby waiting for me to call him with the new date."

"Good girl. So, how's your mom doing?"

"She's doing okay. But she's worried about you."

"What is she worried about?"

"She's worried that you might not come home."

"She thinks that I really killed those people, huh?"

"She won't say, but every time your case pops up on the news, she's glued to the TV, and I even caught her looking it up on her phone."

"Yo, tell her to stop believing the lies those people are putting out there."

"I told her."

"I'll tell her. Where she at?"

"She's home. But she'll be by here later."

"Well, I want to talk to her when I call back."

"Okay, I'll make that happen."

Pricilla and I talked for the remaining time left on my phone call.

After I got off the phone, I turned around to head back into my cell, but I was stopped by this inmate. According to my cellmate, his name was Roman, a middle-aged dude who kept to himself. He equipped himself with a chessboard, handmade chess pieces, and would get into a few games with the old heads in the block on a daily basis. If he was not playing chess, then he was in his cell chilling by himself. He was pretty much a loner, so I was shocked to see him approach me.

"You Zo, right?" he asked.

In stature, Roman was about six-one and weighed about 215 pounds. That was about thirty pounds more than me, but if something were to ever jump off between me and him, I knew I could take him.

"Yeah, what's up?" I replied. I wanted to give off the vibe that I was chill, but possessed an air of confidence, without the cockiness.

"Play chess?" he wanted to know.

"I'm not the best, but I've played a few games."

"Say no more. Let's get into a game," he insisted.

I hesitated for a second, sizing him up, looking at him from head to toe. He noticed it too.

"It's just a casual game of chess. Nothing else," he added.

"He's cool," my cellmate, Wayne, chimed in from the entryway of our cell. He must've heard Roman extend the invitation.

"We playing out here?" I suggested. But it was really more like a request.

"We can," he said.

"A'ight, well, let's do it."

"Let me go and get my chess set," he told me, and then he

headed down to his cell. Less than twenty seconds later, he returned with the board and the chess pieces. After he set up the game, I took a seat on one side of the bench, and he sat down on the opposite side. Moments later, the game began, and in no time, this dude kicked my ass. He beat me in record time of fifteen minutes. I swear, I've never been crucified so quickly in a chess game.

Right after he beat me, he challenged me to a second game, but I opted out of here. And instead we got into a conversation about the politics of the jail and the other inmates in the cell block. He warned me about a few of the guys. Some of them were the same guys my cellmate warned me about, so I took heed. But then the course of the conversation turned toward me. I became the topic of discussion.

"So, is it true that you're in here for murder?" he asked.

"That's what they say," I replied nonchalantly.

"So it ain't true?"

"What, that I did it? Or am I in here for murder?"

"Both."

"Yeah, that's what I'm in here for. But I didn't do it. I didn't kill those old-ass people. Somebody else did it and the cops are trying to put that shit on me."

"Why would they do that?"

"Because they need a fall guy. And I guess I'm that man."

Giving me a suspicious expression, Roman said, "So you mean to tell me, you didn't cash in on all that insurance money them crackers is saying you made off those people?"

"Nah, man, I ain't done none of that shit! I'm innocent on all fronts. I mean, ain't everybody?" I said, cracking a smile. I wanted to bring some laughter into the conversation because Roman was starting to get too personal with this shit. He almost sounded like he was fishing for some information to take back to the cops. I heard around the cell block that this nigga is in here waiting to be sentenced on a drug conviction. They said he got caught with a suitcase of fentanyl in his apartment when the cops raided his spot over a year ago. If everything said was true about this nigga, he could get a minimum of thirty years, being as he's still on parole for another drug and gun charge he was convicted on ten years back. The way I look at it, homeboy is fucked.

He chuckled with me, but it was almost mechanical like. He was more fake than anything. But I let it roll off my shoulders; it was obvious to me that he was playing along to get along. That's survival code around here. I was told that you never show a nigga how you really feeling. That's showing your cards. And you don't wanna do that. You become vulnerable and that's a recipe for disaster in here.

After homeboy laughed with me, I took it as my cue to haul ass to my cell before this conversation turned really sour. I've got a lot of shit on my mind and entertaining this nigga ain't one of them.

So I stood up from the bench and said, "Good game." And then I gave him a dap.

"Maybe we can do this again?" he suggested.

"Yeah, no question. Let's do it," I told him as I began to back away from the table. After taking five steps backward, I was back in my cell with my cellmate and out of view from that weird-ass nigga.

I walked up to my cellmate's bunk and addressed the fact that he cosigned for Roman. "Yo, I thought you said that nigga was good?" I asked him, my mouth tight and barely open. I wanted to be as quiet as possible to prevent anyone on the outside of my cell from hearing me.

My cellie, Wayne, sat up on his bed. "He is good. What happened?" he whispered back.

"The nigga was asking me all types of questions about my case and shit. It almost sounded like he was gathering up information to go back and tell the cops," I expressed sarcastically.

Wayne chuckled. "Nah, Roman is cool. He does everybody like that. He's just trying to feel you out. That's all."

I stepped back from the bunk and tried to rationalize what he'd just said. After mulling it over for a second, I figured that I could be overreacting just a bit. And I could be a little frazzled right now, especially after finding out that Tim was dead. Maybe I needed to sit back and relax for a moment. Regroup before my sister got here later. Maybe it would do me some good. So, without further hesitation, I climbed on my bottom bunk and lay down for a few.

CHAPTER 5

Alayna

I DREADED GOING HOME, BUT I HAD TO. I NEEDED A CHANGE OF clothes, so I had to face Levi, whether I wanted to or not. When I entered my apartment and went into the bedroom, I could tell that he had just gotten out of the shower. He was wrapped in a bath towel, putting on deodorant, when I encountered him.

"Finally decided to come home?" he said sarcastically.

"After that stunt you pulled by giving that agent my phone number, you lucky I came back at all," I stated as I walked over to my walk-in closet.

"You act like I did something wrong. I'm trying to keep your dumb ass out of jail," he roared, and placed the deodorant on the dresser.

"Fuck you, nigga! You're the dumb ass! Riding the federal agents' dicks like you're going to get some kind of badge of honor. You're acting like a real-live snitch right now," I barked at him, and entered my closet.

He stormed inside the closet after me. "Oh, so I'm a snitch now? Don't call me collect when they lock your dumb ass up behind your brother," he warned me, his tone becoming more brass. He was really feeling himself. I swear, I had never seen

25

Levi act this way. He was turning into this other person. It was like he grew a set of balls overnight.

"Trust me, I wouldn't give you the pleasure," I said with authority.

"Oh, so that's it? That's all you have to say?" He wouldn't let up. It was almost like he was starting to badger me.

Before I could utter another word, our doorbell rang. We both turned and looked over our shoulders as if we could see the front door from where we were standing.

"You're expecting someone?" I asked him.

"No."

I instantly got an uneasy feeling in my gut. With everything that was going on, I knew it could be a number of people knocking on my door, and the agent handling my brother's case was at the top of that list.

"You gonna get that?" he wanted to know.

"For what? I don't have anything to say to anyone," I told him.

"Well, I'll get it," he insisted, and immediately slid on a pair of boxer shorts, a pair of jeans and a white T-shirt. He didn't bother putting on any shoes. I continued what I was doing in the closet, because it was only a matter of time before I was out of there.

I can't lie, my heart was racing at an uncontrollable speed the entire time I was back in our bedroom. I tried holding my breath and strained to hear voices coming from the front door, but I couldn't. I even walked out of my closet and stepped into the hallway outside my bedroom door to see if I could hear anything from there, but once again I couldn't. That led me to believe that whoever was at my front door, Levi didn't allow them into the house and made them talk to him from there. If that was the case, this is the first time that idiot did something right.

Unfortunately for me, I spoke too soon, because as soon as I grabbed a few things from my closet and turned around to toss them on the bed, Levi was standing at the doorway of our bedroom with Special Agent McGee and her partner, Special Agent Fletcher. I shook my head with disgust. The sight of Levi and those other monstrosities repulsed me.

"What the fuck is going on, Levi?" I roared, folding my arms across my breast, tapping my feet against the floor as my heart rate picked up speed. Levi saw the rage in my eyes and instantly became nervous.

"They're j-just here to ask you s-some questions, is all," he said, his words stammering. Both agents eyed me down like I was about to go into attack mode.

"I'm not talking to them. Now get them out of my damn house!" I shouted, my voice ricocheting off the walls in my bedroom.

Agent McGee smirked, while her partner stood there and played it cool. "Can you tell us why you were with Tim when he was murdered last night?" she asked me.

This question sent shock waves through the room and Levi was hit first. His face flamed over. His eyes turned red as he spun his head around in slow motion and shot me an evil look. "Tim was murdered last night? And you were there?" he questioned me.

"I'm not going to answer that," I replied gravely.

"Oh, yes, the fuck you are! I am your husband, and once and for all, you are going to listen to me and do what I tell you to do!" he spat.

"Fuck you! You spineless motherfucker! I ain't saying shit to you or them!" I retorted, and then I stormed out of the bedroom with clothes in hand. I didn't even bother to grab a carry-on bag to put my things in. I just wanted to get as far as I could from my husband and those fucking dirtbags with badges.

"Alayna, we know you had something to do with Tim's murder, and those detectives investigating that case are going to nail your ass for it too!" I heard Agent McGee yell out behind me. But her words carried movement, so I knew that she was walking down behind me. Levi and her partner were in tow.

"Alayna, you better get back here right now!" Levi shouted. By this time I had already walked outside the front door and closed it behind me. There was only a five-second delay until I heard both of their voices again.

"Alayna, did your brother order the hit on Tim?" Agent McGee hurled another question at me as I continued on to my car.

I refused to look back at any of them. At that point Levi shot after me. He figured he wasn't going to let me off the hook without a confrontation. I was embarrassing him, and he couldn't take it. He rushed toward me and scurried around the car just as I was about to open the car door. He held out his arm and blocked me from climbing inside.

"Move out of my way, Levi!" I screeched.

"Fuck that! When were you going to tell me that Tim was dead?" He didn't back down.

I tried to push his arm out of the way.

"Move out of my way, Levi!" I demanded.

Now Agents McGee and Fletcher walked up to my car. Once again, they all had me surrounded. "You had Tim killed because he was going to testify against your brother in the insurance fraud case, didn't you?"

I swung my head around in a flash and gave her the look of death. If looks could kill, she would be dead too. "Why don't you ask Tim?" I replied sarcastically, and then I pushed back on Levi really hard, causing him to lose his balance. He tumbled backward a few feet, giving me a small window to hop into my car and lock my door before he could come within arm's reach.

After I had my door secured, I started the ignition and hauled ass out of there. I heard Levi hurl obscenities at my car as I drove away. But I didn't give a damn. As far as I was concerned, he was dead to me. He had sold me out to the cops for the last time and there was no going back. I was done.

* * *

I had no other place to go. I had no friends that I really hung out with. My parents were no longer around, and I only had Alonzo, but he was in jail. So, what was a girl to do? Pricilla's place was my only safe haven right now. And as badly as I wanted to be alone, I couldn't, so her spot was my best bet.

She was shocked to see me come back so soon. "I didn't think I was going to see you again until after you went to visit Zo," she mentioned as she let me into the house.

"I thought so too. But when I went home to unwind, I turned my back for one minute, and when I turned back around, Levi allowed the FBI agents to come into my house and question me about Tim's murder."

"No way. What did you do?"

"I cursed him out, told the agents to kiss my ass, not in so many words, and then I left the house."

"So the agents didn't try to detain you?"

"They couldn't. Tim's case is out of their jurisdiction."

"So, why come to your house?"

"To see if they could catch me out there," I told her as I followed her to the kitchen area of her house.

As soon as I bent the corner, I was in the kitchen, and standing there, pouring herself a glass of wine, was Pricilla's mother. I was shocked to see her mother there; from my understanding she wasn't supposed to be there until later today. Our eyes connected instantly.

"Hey, Mrs. Gates," I greeted her.

"Hey, baby girl. How are you?" she asked.

"I was a little pissed off earlier, but I'm good now."

"Care to talk about it?"

"Rather not."

"Well, I'm sorry to hear about the other firefighter."

"Yeah, I know . . ."

"Tim was his name, right?"

"Yes, ma'am."

"I know it must've been tragic seeing him killed like that?" she questioned me. It wasn't a look of concern. It was more like an act of suspicion. I looked at her ass sideways and then I glanced over at Pricilla, who was standing next to me. She looked at me weird and I knew then she'd had that conversation with her mother. I can't say exactly what she said, but it wouldn't surprise me if she insinuated to her mother that I might have had something to do with Tim's murder. Especially with the way Mrs. Gates questioned me.

I took a deep breath and said, "Yeah, it was devastating. It's haunting me that I couldn't do anything to help him."

"I'm sure," she replied. "So, what exactly happened?"

There was the fifty-million-dollar question: What happened? It felt like I was instantly tossed in an interrogation room with my back against the wall and I had to be very careful of what I said. Mrs. Gates was watching me closely and I knew then she definitely suspected that I had my hands in Tim's murder, so I had to play it safe. I took a deep breath and then I exhaled. "I swear, Mrs. Gates, it all just happened so fast," I started off saying. "We were talking about our relationship. We started disagreeing about something stupid and then two guys appeared out of nowhere and asked him for his wallet. He refused to give it to them, so they shot him and robbed him anyway."

"What were you doing while this was going on?"

"I just stood there in horror."

"Did you scream for help?" Her questions continued.

"Of course, I did. I screamed to the top of my voice, but we were in the middle of nowhere. So, who was going to hear me?"

"Did they try to rob you?"

"No."

"Why not?" she pressed.

"I don't know, Mrs. Gates. Maybe if I see them again, I'll ask them," I replied in a snide manner.

"Don't you find that odd? I mean, you were standing out there with him, right?" Mrs. Gates quipped back. She wasn't backing down.

"I couldn't possibly tell you the story if I wasn't standing out there." My sarcasm grew. In my mind it was apparent she was insinuating that I was behind Tim's robbery. And even though she was right, I wasn't about to make that confession to her.

"Now hold up! Don't get no attitude with me, young lady. I'm just trying to get to the bottom of this thing."

"Well, I'm sorry, but that's just not your job, Mrs. Gates. You need to leave that up to the cops. Let them do their job," I insisted. And I said it in a way to let her know that I didn't appreciate her tone, or her insinuations.

Pricilla heard the irritation in my voice. "Okay, ladies, let's break this up and talk about something else," she suggested nervously.

"Sounds to me that Ms. Alayna here is hiding something," Mrs. Gates barked louder.

I sucked my teeth and shot an evil look at her. "Is there something you really want to say to me?" I got up the gumption to say. I was tired of her back-and-forth innuendos.

"Yes, as a matter of fact I do—" she started off saying, but Pricilla interrupted.

"Mom, now that is enough!" she spat as she stood facing her.

Mrs. Gates pushed back on Pricilla so she could look at me head-on. I was standing only a few feet away. "No, screw that! I'm gonna speak my piece right here and right now," she belted out, and then she followed it with, "Ever since the FBI arrested your brother at the bakery for those murders, I always felt in my heart that something wasn't right with you two . . ."

"Ma, you need to watch what you're saying," Pricilla interjected.

Mrs. Gates pushed her, clean out of the way. "Shut up and get out of my way!" she scolded, and then she started walking toward me. "Now I don't know how much involvement you got in the murders that your brother is being accused of, but I'm most certain that you got something to do with that fellow getting killed last night. Too many people are dying on y'all's watch and it's not a coincidence."

"Mama, now you take that back!" Pricilla shouted.

"I'm not taking shit back! And if you don't wake up and get away from these people, your ass may end up dead next!" she barked at Pricilla.

"Mama, Zo didn't kill those people." Pricilla took up for Alonzo.

"Yes, he did, and you know it. You're just in denial. But DNA doesn't lie. And the sooner you get it in your head that man is a murderer, and he deserves to be where he is, the quicker you could walk away and move on with your life."

"Mama, Alonzo didn't kill those people."

"Shut up, Pricilla! He did kill those people! And you just better be glad that the cops locked his ass up before he killed your ass next," Mrs. Gates blasted Pricilla.

I stood there in awe, but at the same time, I wanted to grab her and choke the shit out of her. I wanted so badly to tell her to shut the fuck up and mind her fucking business. I mean, where was all of this coming from anyway? She wasn't talking shit about my brother when he was paying all her household bills and giving her greedy ass spending money so she could go and game at Rosie's. Oh, but now that the FBI was breathing down my brother's neck and had him locked up in a cage, he was fucking guilty of murder. Fuck her and the boat she came in on. I couldn't wait to tell my brother how she jumped ship on us. She was officially written off with my husband. Fucking traitors!

Instead of chewing Mrs. Gates out, I looked back at Pricilla and asked her if I could use her bathroom to take a quick shower. After she gave me the green light to do so, I immediately made my exit. I heard Mrs. Gates continue to ramble on about her suspicions of me and my brother until I turned on the shower water. After that, every word uttered between Pricilla and her mother was jumbled up and I was okay with it. I would, however, report back to Alonzo about everything that was said today. He would have to know that Mrs. Gates wasn't on our side anymore, and if necessary, she might need to be dealt with.

CHAPTER 6

Pricilla

I COULDN'T WAIT FOR ALAYNA TO GO INTO THE BATHROOM SO I could talk to my mother about her behavior. And as soon as I heard the shower water running, I unleashed a verbal lashing.

"Mom, what has gotten into you?" I started off in a semi-whisper, but my facial expression said it all.

"What do you mean, 'what has gotten into' me? You need to be asking *her* that question, because something isn't right about her," she barked as she stood there with her right hand on her hip. "That crock of shit she fed us just doesn't add up. I mean, how can it be that man got robbed like that and nothing happened to her?"

"Mom, let's not jump to conclusions."

"I'm not jumping to conclusions. I'm only going off what she said. And what she said just doesn't seem right. And I bet those cops investigating the murder are saying the same thing. It isn't no coincidence that man died right before your man has to appear in court." Her voice got louder.

"Now, Mama, you're barking up the wrong tree. Tim getting killed has nothing to do with Alonzo's case. You can just stop that right now."

34

"I'm not gonna stop anything. You better listen to me. I know what I'm talking about, and when the truth comes out, you're going to come back and tell me that I was right."

"That'll be the day," I said, turning my back on her. I grabbed a glass from the cabinet so I could pour some cranberry juice into it.

"So you really don't believe that your man killed those people?"

"No, I don't," I said confidently. "Because I know Alonzo, and I know he is a big teddy bear."

"That's bull! Remember you're my child and I had you. I know when you're lying to me."

"I'm not lying to you," I protested.

My mother started walking toward me. "Oh, yes, you are," she said after she stopped in front of me. "But in there," she added, pressing her pointer finger into my chest cavity, "you know that he killed those people."

"No, I don't . . . I believe him. He won't lie to me, Mama."

"Girl, hush up! Men lie to their girlfriends and wives all the time. What makes you think that you're so different?" she snapped. She wasn't letting up. Her mind was made up. She believed Alonzo killed those people and there was no changing her mind.

"Because I am," I told her, practically slamming the glass down on the island in my kitchen. I had no desire to get anything to drink. I just wanted to get away from her, as far as I could. And my bedroom was going to have to do the trick for now.

CHAPTER 7

Kirsten

*I*FINALLY GOT UP THE GUMPTION TO LEAVE THE HOUSE AND TAKE A trip over to the station to talk to the guys who worked for my husband. I was more than sure they knew Tim was dead. I mean, the incident had been televised a few times, and since no one called me to check on his whereabouts, I figured the cops must've paid them a visit.

I was hoping to get there between field calls. When I drove up and saw a couple of the guys hanging outside talking, I was relieved to see that I had gotten there at the right time.

"Hi, guys," I greeted the three men after I had gotten out of my car. They were standing near the picnic table a few feet away from the parking lot. I immediately recognized all three of them and forced myself to smile as I approached them.

"Hi, Mrs. Stancil," Paul spoke first.

"Yeah, how you doing?" Mike spoke next.

Jesse smiled and gave me a head nod. I nodded back at him.

"Hi, you guys," I finally returned the pleasantries.

"So, what brings you here?" Paul wanted to know.

He was acting like he was feeling me out, trying to see if I knew about Tim yet. Or he could've been checking my temperature to see how well I took the news of Tim being murdered. Who knew what he was doing, but I was sure I would find out sooner rather than later.

"I came to check on you guys. To see how you're holding up," I said.

"So you know?" Jesse blurted out.

I smiled. "Of course, I know, silly. The detectives stopped by my home late last night and broke the news to me."

"Oh, man, Mrs. Stancil, I am so sorry for your loss!" Paul immediately apologized.

"Yeah, me too," Mike volunteered.

"I appreciate that, you guys."

"So, how are the kids taking it?" Paul wanted to know.

"They aren't taking it so well. They're sitting at home now with my mother and their aunt on Tim's side."

"I'm sorry to hear that. Death is hard on kids," Mike added.

"So, what did the cops say?" Jesse chimed in.

I took a deep breath and exhaled. "They pretty much said that Tim met Alayna at a salvage junkyard so that they could talk about their relationship, and then some guys popped out of nowhere. They robbed and killed him."

"They told us the same thing," Paul stated.

"For the life of me, I can't figure out why they would meet at that junkyard, at that time of the night," Mike wanted to know.

"Because she asked him to meet her there," Jesse chimed back in.

"And how do you know this?" I probed Jesse.

"Because before he left, he told me that's where he was going. And I tried to talk him out of it, but he wouldn't listen."

"What did you say to him?" I prodded some more.

"I said, 'I don't like the idea of you leaving the station this time of night to go and meet her.' I told him that I didn't trust her, especially after everything that happened when you came to the office. And then I told him that if he really had to meet her, he should tell her to come here. But he wouldn't listen and left anyway."

"So you had a bad feeling about it?"

"Yes, I did. And look, I was right."

"I want your honest opinion. Do you think that Alayna had something to do with Tim's death?" I looked at all three men standing before me.

Jesse spoke first. "Of course, I do," he spoke confidently.

"Oh, come on, we don't know that for sure," Paul spoke up.

"Yeah, let's not jump to conclusions. Let's let the detectives do their job before we pass judgment," Mike suggested.

But I wasn't feeling his answer or Paul's. I agreed with Jesse one hundred percent. He was onto something, and it seemed like he knew more than these other guys. It also seemed like he had a closer relationship with Tim than Paul and Mike had. So my best bet was to keep in contact with Jesse so he could keep me plugged in with what was going on around the station. He could be my eyes and ears.

"Has anyone seen Alayna since yesterday?" I asked everyone.

"No, she hasn't stopped by here," Paul replied.

"I haven't seen her either," Mike said.

"She knows not to show her face around here," Jesse added.

"What about Alonzo? Do any of you guys talk to him?" I continued with my questions.

"Not since he's been in jail," Paul answered.

"I haven't spoken to him either," Mike declared.

"I didn't talk to him when he was out of jail." Jesse was pulling it out.

"Do you guys believe that he has something to do with those murders?" I questioned them.

"As far as I'm concerned, the jury is still out on that one," Paul commented.

"I have no comment either way," Mike said.

"Well, I do," Jesse stated with conviction.

Jesse's bluntness piqued my interest. I needed to hear what he had to say. "I'm listening," I encouraged him.

"If you want my honest opinion, I believe with all my heart that he killed those people, and Tim believed the same thing," he explained.

"Did Tim tell you that?"

"Yes, we talked about it several times," Jesse added.

"Did Tim share this with you guys too?" I asked Mike and Paul.

Paul answered first. "We talked about it, but he never came out and said that he believed Alonzo committed the murders."

"Yeah, we talked about it too, but like with Paul, he never actually said that he believed Alonzo did it. In my honest opinion, I don't think that he really wanted to believe that Alonzo would do something like that," Mike stated.

"Well, he told me just the opposite. And we both agreed that all the evidence the detectives gathered pointed directly at Alonzo. I believe that Alayna knows her brother did it. And I also believe that she knew Tim was talking to the cops about it, so she had to get rid of him."

"Aww . . . come on now, Jesse! You don't know that for sure!" Paul interjected. He made it very apparent that he disagreed with Jesse's accusation.

Mike stood there in disbelief.

"Well, I also believe that she had him killed because she felt like if she couldn't have him, no one could," Jesse continued.

I watched Paul's and Mike's facial expressions and they both cringed. Paul even threw his hands up. "I've heard enough," he said, and then he walked off. Mike said nothing, but joined him.

That didn't stop Jesse from talking, though, and I listened.

"They don't want to face the reality that Tim was ambushed, and it was all at the hands of Alayna."

"So you knew about the affair?" I questioned him.

"Yes, I did."

"How long were they seeing each other?"

"I can't say."

"So, when did you first hear about it?"

"Right after I started working here."

"Did Tim ever tell you that he loved her?"

"Oh, no, Mrs. Stancil. And I don't even think he did."

"Well, what do you think it was?"

"Just someone to pass the time with. And I also believe that she wanted more from him, and he wasn't willing to give it to her."

"Did those other guys know about the affair?"

"I don't think so."

"What about Alonzo? Think he knew?"

"No, he didn't know. As a matter of fact, he found out right after you did. You know the day that you found them two in the office when you stopped by?"

"Yes."

"Well, that's when Zo found out and he was angry. Tim told me that Zo felt betrayed by it, being that Alayna was his little sister and Tim watched her grow up."

"You heard him say that?"

"Not in so many words, yes."

"In your opinion, do you believe that Tim loved me?" I asked. With everything said in these last ten minutes, I needed to hear that in spite of everything, my husband loved me.

"No doubt. Mrs. Stancil, there was not a day that Tim didn't talk about you. He adored you and the kids," Jesse assured me.

And I must say that it warmed my heart to hear him utter those words. I hated what my husband did to me, but I loved him no less, because he was a good man and a loving father to his children.

"I really appreciate you saying that, Jesse."

"Anytime, Mrs. Stancil. But I wish that Tim was here to tell you himself."

"I wish he was too," I agreed.

Jesse and I spoke a little more about what he knew concerning Tim's murder. I suggested to him to keep me in the loop, especially if he saw or heard something that would help bring Tim's killers to justice. After he agreed to do so, I gave him a hug and thanked him. I started to leave and return home, but I decided to go into Tim's office and clear out some of his things.

Inside of his office, nothing looked out of place. I saw our wedding photos placed on the right side of his desk. One of our camping trip photos, which he and I and the kids took last summer, placed next to it. The glass 8-Ball I purchased as one of his birthday gifts a few years back was sitting next to a stack of incident reports. I sat down behind his desk and started sifting through those reports. I was very curious to see if anything looked amiss in them. See if I could point out any inconsistency. Find out exactly what my husband had going on with Alonzo and how deep he really was in this mess. I swear, I wished I had known when all of this first started happening, because if I had had any knowledge of it, I would've shut it down immediately. And Tim would probably still be alive right now.

As I was going through his things, I came across sticky notes with phone numbers of women written on them. I paused for a moment, wondering if he had affairs with them too. After quickly dismissing that notion, I found a birthday card from Alayna wishing Tim a happy thirty-ninth birthday. I instantly got sick to my stomach after reading the first line: *Happy 39th Birthday, Love!* And then the card read:

> *I've loved you from the first time we kissed. And even though it's only been a couple of years now since we've been*

together, it seems like it's been a lifetime. I look forward to spending this happy occasion with you and ending the night with a bang.

    See you later!

    XOXO!

    Alayna

My heart began to ache as I thought back to the day in question. I remember Tim's thirty-ninth birthday like it was yesterday. He had to work here at the station, so the kids and I brought him a birthday cake to celebrate his day. After we sang "Happy Birthday," we sat around and ate ice cream and cake, and then we left him here to work. It broke my heart to know that he slept with Alayna later that night.

How could he do that to me? And to know that she had been sleeping with my husband all that time and smiling in my face like we were friends. Fucking bitch!

I was gonna see her soon, and when I did, I was gonna let her have it.

CHAPTER 8

Alonzo

"*R*IDDICK, GET READY, YOU GOT A VISITOR," I HEARD THE CO
shout from the front of the cell block. I was sitting on the metal
bench playing a game of chess with Roman when I heard my
name. I looked at Roman, and before I could utter one word, he
gave me the green light to handle my business. "Just come to my
cell and let me know when you get back," he instructed me
while I was getting up from the table.

"A'ight," I replied, and then I headed over to the cell bars.

"Open cell block 8-B," the CO radioed the command pod.
Several seconds later, the door slid open. I stepped in the small
cage and watched the door close. Immediately the cell door on
the opposite side of me opened, which allowed me to step into
the hallway.

"Turn toward the wall," the CO ordered.

After I turned and faced the wall, he handcuffed my wrists behind my back and then he led me out of the cell block into a
nearby corridor. The path of that corridor led us to the visiting
room. When I entered the small, cramped visiting area, I looked
around and for the first time noticed the sad faces on all of the
women there visiting the other men, all speaking in hushed tones.

43

The entire scene was depressing. There was no way I could live out the rest of my life in this hellhole, knowing this was the only way I'd be able to see and communicate with my loved ones. I had to get out of here.

Immediately after I figured that I had seen enough, I turned my attention toward my sister, Alayna, who was sitting on a stoop behind the Plexiglas partition. She smiled as soon as we locked eyes. I smiled back at her and whispered that I loved her, all while the CO was uncuffing me. The second he released me from the handcuffs, I sat down on the stoop across from her and grabbed the telephone receiver from the wall on my side of the booth. She grabbed her phone too and greeted me.

"What's up, bro?" she said.

"You tell me." And even though I wanted her to fill me in on what was going on out there in the streets, she knew she had to be extra careful with the words she used, since the phone we were on had recording devices on them.

"I'm just taking it easy," she started off.

I could see the look in her eyes. Clearly, she had something weighing heavily on her mind. Right now would be the perfect time to be able to read minds.

"As you should," I replied. "So, how are you doing?"

"I've had better days," she commented.

"You know, I can't believe that Tim is gone," I said. I had to break the ice, because she acted like she was afraid to do so.

She shook her head back and forth and then sighed heavily. "You know I love you, right?"

"Yeah," I said hesitantly. I wondered where she was going with this.

"And everything I do, I do for you . . ." She looked down at her lap.

"So, what are you saying?" I pressed her.

She glanced back up, but instead of uttering another word,

44

she started using sign language. She started off with the word "I" and then she formed the words "had Tim killed."

I sat up in the chair and looked at her strangely. One part of me wasn't surprised, but then again, it kind of shocked me she had the balls to do something like that. I needed to know more.

I started using sign language to respond to her. I asked why she did it, and she began to tell me that Tim had made a deal with the Feds to bury me underneath the jail, and she wasn't going to allow that to happen. Then she threw up the "I Love You to Death" hand signs and then she finished it off by signing: "And I refuse to let anyone do anything that would take you away from me. So, I did what needed to be done."

Tears started streaming down her face and I immediately placed my right hand on the Plexiglas partition that separated us. "I love you, Alayna. And I would do the same shit for you! Don't you ever forget it!"

She started wiping the tears from her face with the back of her hands and then she cleared her throat.

"So you're not upset with me?" She started using sign language again.

"Fuck no! I'm proud of you. What you did took balls!" I blurted out, forgetting that I was supposed to respond back by using my hands.

Alayna smiled. I could see that I had brightened her mood.

"You know I would've done the same thing for you, right?" I told her via sign language. I wanted to make sure that she didn't regret for a second what she did for me.

She raised her hands and started forming the words "I know you would!"

I smiled back and formed the question "Who else knows about this?"

Her reply was "No one."

I signed, "Good, keep it that way. It's our little secret."

She smiled once again. This gave me the impression that she was starting to feel just a little better, and this made me feel good. And as badly as I wanted to drop the subject before one of the COs came through here and saw what we were doing, I wanted to know who pulled the trigger. Who were the gunmen that the news media was inquiring about?

So I positioned my hands and formed the words "Who did you get to do the job?"

She hesitated for a second before raising her hands and forming "K-Rock and Russell."

I must admit that I was taken aback by her answer. But I was curious to know, why them? Why get them to murder Tim? So, as I motioned my arms, making hand gestures, I asked her. And her answer, "Because they were the only ones I could trust outside of you. I knew they would get the job done and not tell the cops." Then she put her hands down just in the nick of time because the CO walked into the visiting room behind me with another inmate in tow. Alayna looked all shook up, so I calmly asked her to put a smile on her face.

She smiled like I instructed her to do, and I started up a verbal conversation so that we could appear normal. "Whatcha eat today?" I spoke into the telephone receiver as the CO escorted the inmate by me.

"I got a veggie wrap and a smoothie from Tropical Smoothie a couple of hours ago."

"Oh, yeah, I like those. But you should've gotten the grilled chicken wrap with the mango habanero sauce. That one is good."

"Remember, I introduced you to that wrap," she pointed out.

After she jogged my memory, I said, "Oh, yeah, you did hook me up with that wrap."

"What are they feeding you in here?" she wanted to know.

"A bunch of shit. Boiled eggs and cold-ass bread in the morning. Mystery meat, mustard packs, and bread in the afternoon, and mystery meat covered in gravy and nasty-ass mashed potatoes for dinner."

"What time is dinner?"

"They feed us around five-thirty. And the food portions are like elementary school trays, so by the time seven o'clock rolls around, you're hungry again. Guys who can't afford commissary are going through it in this place. It's hard."

"Been in any fights?"

I chuckled. "Of course not. Ain't none of those guys back there crazy enough to pick a fight with me."

"Okay, tough guy," she joked. "Have you seen any fights?"

"I've seen one of the young boys get roughed up a little for talking shit to an old head. But other than that, it's been pretty chill."

"So, whatcha do to pass the time?"

"Watch TV and play chess."

"Play chess?"

"Yeah, I play with this guy named Roman. And he's good too. He's taught me a few tricks here and there."

"That's nice," she said, looking back over both of her shoulders. When she turned back around to face me, she lifted her hands and started using sign language again. She started off with the words "Don't be surprised if some cops come here and ask you about Tim's murder."

I replied to her by forming the words "I already know and I'm gonna be ready for them. Don't you even worry."

Alayna smiled and exhaled, and then she made more hand gestures and formed the words "I don't trust Levi anymore. And I would have him done too if I didn't think the cops would be breathing down my neck."

Shocked by her message, I signed, "Be careful, li'l sis. I don't need you getting your hands dirty anymore. Let me handle things from here."

She thought about what I said for a moment and then she nodded her head in agreement.

With only ten minutes left in the visit, Alayna and I talked about other things, like Pricilla and how she was holding up. And then she dropped the bomb on me and told me that Mrs. Gates was throwing salt at me.

"She's not on our side, big bro," she told me.

"I know. I sensed that after a couple of days sitting in here. I heard her a few times talking shit in the background when I was on the phone with Pricilla. I told Pricilla to tell her to shut the fuck up. But Pricilla wouldn't tell her, though."

"When I was over there earlier, she started questioning me about Tim's murder. Wanted to know why I wasn't shot when Tim was."

"What did you tell her?"

"I told her I didn't know, because everything happened so fast, but she wasn't trying to hear it, and I wasn't trying to hear her, so I got out of there."

"You know, I don't want her at my wedding."

"I don't blame you. She's a piece of work. But Pricilla isn't going to have it."

"The way I feel now, Pricilla better hope that we still get married."

"Keep in mind that your deposits aren't refundable," Alayna reminded me.

"I don't give a fuck about those deposits. I'm more concerned about beating these murder raps. Outside of that, nothing else matters."

"I feel you," she answered.

We continued chatting until the CO broke up our conversation. "Visitations are over," he announced, so I said goodbye to Alayna and stood up from the metal stool. We blew each other a kiss and then we both walked away from each other.

* * *

Back in the cell block, I sat down with Roman and finished our game of chess. "How was your visit?" he asked.

"It was great. Got a chance to sit down and really bond with my baby sister."

"How old is she?"

"Twenty-seven."

"She's young."

"Yeah, and she's my world too. The only person I've got left."

"What do you mean, 'the only person' you 'got left'?"

"Both of my parents are dead. They only had me and my little sister. So she's all I've got."

"You got kids?"

"Nope."

"Nieces or nephews?"

"Nope."

"Come on, man, whatcha doing? You suppose to have some kids to carry on your name."

"Yeah, I'll work on that when I get out of here."

"So you think you're getting out of here?"

"You fucking right I am. I'm gonna beat my charges."

"Murder, right?"

"Yeah."

"Three counts, right? Man, how the fuck you gon' beat that?"

"Because I didn't do it."

"So you innocent?"

"You damn right I am. I didn't kill those old-ass people. And besides, they probably had one foot in the grave anyway," I commented, and then I chuckled.

Roman looked at me weird, but then he burst into laughter. It kind of struck me as odd, being that his laughter seemed forced. But then again, this could be who this guy was. I mean, maybe he didn't realize how funny my joke was until the last minute? Or maybe the nigga was slow?

"Well, whoever killed those people really did them in. Because I heard there was so much blood in the married couple's house that bloody footprints were all over the place."

"Who told you that?" I questioned. He was acting like he had an inside track. Or maybe he knew someone down in forensics. Shit, this guy could be police on the low. But then again, if he were undercover, he wouldn't have ever admitted to hearing about how gory the murder scene was. Maybe I was just being paranoid or something, but I did need him to tell me who his source was.

"The news. Everybody in here heard the news. People say how bloody the house was when the cops and the paramedics went inside to get them."

I let out a sigh of relief when I heard Roman's answer. He was right, the news outlets have made that report a few times. I heard it with my own ears.

"Where did you think I heard it?" he questioned me.

"I don't know. That's why I asked you," I replied. At that moment I had just realized that from the time we started talking about Alayna and then the murders, we hadn't moved one chess piece. Roman was so engrossed in my conversation that he took his attention off the game totally.

"Whatcha think, I'm one of those niggas looking to get a confession out of you so I could go home earlier?"

I burst into laughter because this dude was really onto something. He either knew how to read minds, or I must've stepped on his toes. "Shit, I don't know. Are you?" I replied, and waited for him to answer.

"All these niggas in this cell block can vouch for me. I ain't no snitch! You can best believe that," he told me. He poked out his chest when he said it too. His mannerisms made me believe that he was a man of honor. But then you got to remember that you're in jail. And niggas that have come in here, have come from all walks of life, so they could be anyone they wanted to be. So you could never be too sure.

"Yeah, a'ight. You got it," I insisted, because I didn't want to go there with him.

He said that he wasn't a snitch and the guys in here could vouch for him, then so be it. I refused to go back and forth with a dude I didn't know. It's counterproductive. As a matter of fact, I was gonna finish this game and then retire to my cell. I had a lot of stuff on my mind that I needed to figure out. And I couldn't do it and entertain this dude at the same time. It would be impossible.

"Let's finish this game so I can go and lie down," I told him.

I was glad he got the message because he didn't say another word. He put his head back in the chess game and moved his next piece. I followed suit.

CHAPTER 9

Alayna

AFTER I LEFT THE JAIL FROM VISITING MY BROTHER, I FELT BETTER. It felt like a weight had been lifted off my shoulders after telling him that I had Tim murdered. I was so happy to know that he wasn't upset with me. It was also good to hear him say that he would've done the same for me. I am definitely my brother's keeper. We will have one another's back forever.

Once back inside my car, I realized that I couldn't go home, nor could I go back to Pricilla's place, so I decided to get a hotel room for the night and figure out things from there. Besides, I needed to be alone right now anyway, especially with everything that was going on. I needed to figure some shit out before all of this stuff consumed me.

I knew that we already decided against it, but I really needed to take a ride over to K-Rock's place and have a talk with him. The other hit he was supposed to do hadn't been done yet. I hadn't seen shit on the news broadcasting it and time was running out. What was the holdup? What was his plan? Had he backed out of it? Gotten cold feet? Or had he just said fuck it and walked away with my money? I swear, he'd better hope that he didn't screw me around with this because I would make his life a living hell. Alonzo didn't like his ass anyway. So, if he found out that K-Rock jerked me out of that cash, Zo would have something done to him and his whack-ass friend. Pricilla would be one brother short for this year's family portrait.

Speaking of Pricilla, I wondered how she'd feel if she knew that her brother murdered someone to get her fiancé out of jail? Would she go along with it, or would she rat us out? I guessed it all depended on how deep her love was for her brother versus the pressure the cops would put on her if they figured out she knew something. That whole scenario would end badly, with everyone behind bars. So I continued to say, the less she knew, the better off everyone would be. That included me.

As far as K-Rock's friend Russell, I didn't know too much about him, but I hoped he could keep his mouth closed too. I've heard stories where a negro has fucked a chick and afterward took part in pillow talk, and that's when the idiot started bragging about hits he's made. And the whole time homegirl was looking to cash in on the 1-800 hotline for the measly one-thousand-dollar check the city gave to Crime Stoppers. The whole shit was bogus, but people did it all the time.

Five minutes into my drive, I decided to go to the Hyatt Place on Independence Boulevard in Virginia Beach. I was literally across from Pembroke Mall. I was away from everyone. And this was exactly what I needed.

After I checked in, I was given a room on the seventh floor overlooking Town Center. The view was beautiful, but it didn't give me any peace of mind. As a matter of fact, I was beginning to feel lonely. Alonzo mentioned earlier during the visit that I wasn't in this alone. But that couldn't be further from the truth, because right now I felt like I was by myself. There was no telling when or if I was going to ever feel different about it. Until Alonzo came home, I was out here alone. My husband, Levi, and everyone else had seemed to have switched sides on me. What moves could I take to keep the cops from getting tipped off that I murdered Tim? As much as I was beginning to regret doing it now, it was too late. The damage was done.

So what I gotta do now was keep my nose clean and stay two steps ahead of everyone who could put me behind bars. What would that be? What would I do? I didn't know.

CHAPTER 10

Jesse

After calling Alayna's cell phone for two days and not getting an answer, I decided to pull up to her apartment. I was going to get to the bottom of what really happened the night she met up with Tim. I wasn't going to stand for her lies, like the detectives were. There was a new sheriff in town and I was going to show her who was in charge.

Her car wasn't parked nowhere in the vicinity, so it was evident she wasn't home. But that didn't stop my plans. I was going to sit there and wait for her to show up. I sat in my car and watched her apartment for three hours, starting at sunrise, and what do you know? The heffa finally decided to show up.

Immediately after she parked and exited her car, I was in tow and practically on her heels. She didn't see me walking behind her until I announced my presence.

"Good morning, Alayna! Can I have a word with you?" I started off as I trailed her down a long sidewalk toward her apartment building.

"Leave me alone. I have nothing to say to you," she replied as she continued down the sidewalk.

"Oh, but, yes, you do," I insisted. I needed to talk to her about

Tim's murder—and she was going to stop and talk to me. She owed me that much.

Alayna stopped and turned around to face me. "What do you want with me?"

"I want to know what happened the night you met up with Tim," I didn't hesitate to say.

"I've already told the cops what happened, so I'm not going to repeat myself," she replied. Then she turned around and started to walk away, but I reacted by grabbing her arm before she could get away from me.

"You better keep your fucking hands off me, you freak!" Alayna hissed, pushing my hands back roughly. Her reaction was so swift, it felt like a venomous snake had leapt back at me and bitten my hand. That, in turn, caused me to hit my nose with my own hand. It stung like hell. I immediately had to pinch the bridge of my nose trying to quell the throbbing that had suddenly started between my eyes.

"Why did you do that?" I said gruffly, still trailing her, but, at the same time, looking around to see if anyone had noticed the altercation between us. It was safe to say that no one was around. At least from where I was standing.

"If you don't stop following me, I'm going to call the police," Alayna warned me.

"Call 'em!" I dared her. "And while you're at it, tell 'em you killed Tim!" I shouted.

"I swear, Jesse! You better leave me alone, if you know what's good for you," she threatened as she continued to walk ahead of me. But this time she was within a couple feet of her front door. I knew it was now or never if I wanted to get everything off my chest.

"You can run all you want. But you and I both know that you had Tim killed because he didn't want you anymore. You figured that if you couldn't have him, no one else was going to either."

I must've struck a nerve because after I spewed those words out at Alayna, her head spun around like the girl in *The Exorcist*. She stomped back over to me and, in a knee-jerk reaction, slapped me in the face. I held my cheek in shock.

"You fucking bitch!" I spat.

"No, you're the bitch! Tim was bending you over like a cheap fucking whore. I wonder what his wife would say if she knew you two were fucking?"

"Fuck you! Tim loved me! And you know it, that's why you had him killed!" I screeched. I needed to let her know that I knew the truth, regardless of what it appeared like.

Alayna chuckled loudly. "Sucking his dick behind closed doors is what you call *love*? Jesse, blow me! You're fucking insane!"

"No, bitch, you're insane! And when I find out that you had something to do with Tim's murder, I'm going straight to the cops, and when they come and lock you up, I'm going to be front and center."

"You better watch yourself!" she threatened, and then she turned and walked off slowly. The look in her eyes was deadly.

"So, is that a threat?" I shouted. "You're gonna have someone kill me next?" I shouted louder. But she ignored me and continued to her house. "I know you hear me, heffa!" I shouted once more, until she closed the front door of her apartment.

I didn't realize that I had dozed off to sleep when I went back to the station, until my cell phone rang. "Hello," I huffed into the mouthpiece, my eyes still half-shut. "Hello?" I grumbled, and still got no response. But then I held my breath for a second and that's when I heard someone breathing on the other end of the line. My eyes suddenly popped open when I finally heard a voice.

"You're a dead man, fucking fag!" the gruff voice on the other end growled.

The shrill threats coming through the phone incited fear in me, so much that I immediately disconnected the call. I even powered if off, preventing the caller from calling me back.

"Who the fuck was that?" I murmured after I snatched the phone away from my ear and peered at the screen frantically after I powered it back on. The call read **UNKNOWN.** The fact that I didn't recognize the voice frazzled me. I sat up in the bed and scrubbed my hands over my face; then I exhaled and looked at my phone one more time as if something had changed.

"Oh, my God! Whoever killed Tim is going to kill me next." I panicked and hopped out of bed.

I rushed to the door of my room and snatched it open. With my phone clutched so tight that the veins on the top of my hand bulged against the skin, I headed into the bathroom and flicked on the lights above the sink. I stared at myself in the large mirror hanging over the sink. I could see the worry flickering in my own eyes as I thought about the fact that I had no idea of who the caller was, but the possibilities were endless. That thought alone caused a shiver to run down the length of my spine.

It was becoming unbearable and all I could do was whisper to myself, "What am I going to do now?"

I really felt like the best solution was to call the detectives handling Tim's murder case. I was sure they'd guide me in the right direction. Maybe even provide me with some protection. Have a patrol car tail me when I left to go home. If not, and I found out the death threats were real, then I was fucked! And I couldn't have that. I had a whole life ahead of me and I wanted to live.

KNOCK! KNOCK! KNOCK!

Startled by the sudden clatter on the bathroom door, I flinched. Seconds later, I managed to ask who was on the other side of the door. I exhaled a sigh of relief when I found out that it was Mike.

"Hey, how long are you going to be in there?"

"I'll be out in a minute," I assured him. Not even a moment later, I had opened the bathroom door to let him in. He stood face-to-face with me.

"Hey, you all right?" he asked.

"As a matter of fact, I'm not. I think someone is going to try to kill me."

Mike burst into laughter. "Who's gonna try and kill you?" he asked in disbelief. He acted as if I was pulling his leg or something.

"Mike, this isn't funny. I just got a phone call, and someone threatened to kill me," I told him.

"Well, then you better call the cops and report it," he suggested, patting me on the shoulders before easing by me so he could get into the bathroom. After he was inside, he closed the bathroom door behind him. So much for getting the help of a fellow coworker.

CHAPTER 11

Alayna

*I*SNICKERED UNTIL MY FACE TURNED BLUE AFTER I DISCONNECTED the call from Jesse's scary ass. Downloading the app to disguise my voice was the best thing I could've ever done. Who would've thought that Mr. Tough Guy would become all scared and shit over a phone call? Just a few days ago, he grew a set of balls and brought his ass over to my house to harass me about something he knew nothing about. He was confronting *me* over Tim's death. And then he took it another step further by getting in my face and grabbing me. But I shut him down that instant. And it took me another ten minutes to get rid of him, but I did it.

After he left, I thought that I was over it. But I wasn't, so I had to figure out a way to get this moron back. Get him back in a way where he'd think first before deciding he wanted to come to my house and bully me. That's where the voice generator app came into play. It was the best idea I could've ever come up with. But what was more rewarding was hearing this bastard's voice tremble on the other end of the phone after I began to threaten him. All he wanted to know was who I was, sounding traumatized with each word he uttered from his mouth. He was a fucking pussy and I proved that just by one little prank call. That was all it took.

I started to torture him a little bit longer, but if I had kept him on the phone one minute more, I probably would've laughed. That's just how funny this whole thing was. All that badass talk he had the other day went right out the window as soon as I uttered the words "You're a dead man, fucking fag!" At that moment he lost all sense of reality and all the manhood he had left in his body. And to know that I caused this made me feel like I had won that battle.

With a feeling of vindication running through my veins, I placed my cell phone down near my pillow. I grabbed the remote control to unmute the television, but my cell phone rang, and it startled me. I picked it back up and looked at the caller ID. It was Levi calling me. I started not to answer, but then I figured that he might be having car troubles or maybe was at his mother's house and wanted to know if I wanted him to bring me a dinner plate, since she cooked every single day.

"Hello," I said reluctantly.

"Hey, what are you doing?"

"Lying down, watching TV. Why?"

"Oh, nothing. I'm over my mom's house and I wanted to let you know that the detective investigating Tim's case just left here a few minutes ago."

Shocked by what he was saying, I sat straight up in bed. "How did he know where your mother lives?" I questioned him, my heart beginning to race at a rapid speed. It seemed like the tables had turned at that moment. Now it was my nerves being rattled.

"I don't know."

"What did they say?" I asked.

"They said they wanted to talk to me alone, so Mom went into her bedroom while I talked to them in the den."

"Okay, and what did they say?" I pressured him because he wasn't giving anything. If he was in front of me, I'd probably grab him by the arm and twist it.

"They wanted to know what kind of relationship you and I had. Had you ever threatened to hurt or kill me? And are you capable of ordering a hit on someone?" he finally said, his words rushing out like a rapid waterfall.

I started shaking my head, up and down, while contemplating what question to ask him next. And then it came to me: "And what did you say?" At this point I was concerned with what Levi told them.

"I told them that we argued from time to time, but that was about the size of it."

"Is that it? Because you're talkative and I know you had something else to say." I didn't ask him; I stated it more like a fact. I believed that he said a lot more than what he was trying to let on.

"Honestly, they did most of the talking . . ." he began to say, but I knew it was straight bullshit. I've had my share of interrogations with homicide detectives, and I knew that they did the least talking in interviews. They were more interested in what the person they were interviewing had to say.

"Come on now, Levi, who do you think you're fooling? Stop with all the lies. I know those cops came there to hear what you had to say, not the other way around. So keep it one hundred with me and tell me what you said."

I fired off accusations in rapid succession, and while doing so, it felt like my skin was seemingly stretching out tightly with worry lines. I only allowed this to happen when I was alone and under pressure. I wouldn't allow myself to be this visibly worried in front of authorities because it would be a dead giveaway.

"Well, I'm sorry that you don't believe me, but it's true," he griped.

I knew he was lying, but he wasn't backing down. He was going to hold on to his story for dear life.

"You know what, if you're going to sit on this phone and lie to me about a conversation you had with the cops, I refuse to listen to it. Especially when you got a track record of throwing me underneath the bus to these fucking cops. I'm your wife and lately you've been feeding me to the wolves."

"What? She doesn't believe you or something?" I heard his mother saying in the background.

Hearing her voice lit a flame underneath me. My eyes fluttered and my head started spinning. It seemed like everything around me was going in circular motion. I couldn't tell you if I was coming or going. My ears started ringing and then my head felt like someone had it in a vise grip. It was all too much.

"You tell her to mind her fucking business!" I roared.

"I'm not telling her anything and you need to watch your mouth. You don't be disrespecting my mother!" his voice screeched.

I could feel the heat coming through the phone. He hated when I talked about his mother. It ate at his soul. But I hated it when his mother always intervened in our marital disputes. She had no filter. And he did nothing to prevent her from doing it.

"Fuck her! And fuck you too! Calling me with all that bullshit talk about the detectives stopped by to speak with you about me. I know damn well you probably called them to find out what was going on. Because how is it they knew where your mother lived? That just doesn't sound right to me."

"Well, you can believe what you want. I know that I didn't call the detectives. They came here on their own."

"So she thinks that you called the cops over here?" his mother's voice rang out again. The sound of her voice felt like a Brillo pad scraping against my arm.

"Tell her, yes, I do. Because both of y'all motherfuckers are as noisy as they come," I spat. My blood pressure was rising with every word I spewed forth from my mouth.

"Why don't you just worry about trying to stay out of jail. Because from what I heard, they're dead on your ass, you whore!"

"'Whore'?!" I screamed.

"Yeah, *whore*! You fucked a married man for two years, and when I asked you whether or not y'all were having an affair, you lied in my face and made me think I was crazy for even asking you. But guess what? I was right the entire time. So, as far as I see it, whatever you got coming to you, you deserve it."

"Oh, really?"

"Yeah, really."

"Well, let me tell you something, *you two-minute man*. Tim was more of a man than you could've ever been. He was loved and respected. He was a boss and he had men looking up to him. He ran shit around the station, and he knew his stuff, so that's what turned me on about him. He was important, unlike you. I mean, what do you have going for you? A gym teacher's T-shirt with your name on it and a bunch of fucking smelly kids running around the school gym with no athletic abilities. Let's face it, Levi, you're a loser, just like the kids you babysit. And that's why I snuck around behind your back and fucked Tim. He made me feel alive and he gave me things. Showered me with money and gifts, something you obviously can't do . . ." My voice trailed off.

"Yeah, you loved him so much that you had him killed, huh?" he struck back.

I instantly became enraged and blew my top. "I didn't have him killed!" I snapped.

"Why don't you convince the cops of that," he stated sarcastically, and then he abruptly disconnected our call. And just like that, the phone line went dead.

I sat there with my cell phone in my hand and thought all sorts of mean thoughts of Levi. But the two words that exited my mouth were, "That motherfucker!"

CHAPTER 12

Kirsten

DEALING WITH THE REALIZATION THAT TIM WAS NO LONGER WITH me and the kids brought a lot of turmoil upon my family. My kids were taking it pretty bad. My daughter was having nightmares, while my son, T.J., was taking out his anger on the kids in the neighborhood. Just yesterday my neighbor around the corner called and told me that my son attacked hers during a one-on-one game of basketball. She said that T.J. elbowed her son in the face after he lost the game. I was shocked at first, because that's not the type of behavior my son displayed in public. When I asked him about it, he brushed it off like it was nothing and proceeded to his bedroom. I was thrown for a loop. He has been taking this very hard, and I might end up having to get him some counseling pretty soon.

Feeling all this pain had fueled me to make a trip to see Alayna. I told my mother about my plans to do this, but she repeatedly told me not to go there. But seeing the hurt in my children's eyes wouldn't allow me to let this one slide. Alayna needed to see my face after what she'd done to me and my kids. She needed to know the hurt she caused, and I was going to personally let her know that I would certainly see to it that she got the maximum sentence allowed by the courts, when the cops found out she was behind my husband's murder.

When I was going through my husband's things at the office, I ran across her home address in her profile folder, which was filed away with the other firefighters' information.

I sat in my car and waited for an hour before I got up the gumption to go and knock on her door. I was surprised to see her greet me with a smile after she opened the door and saw that it was me.

"What a pleasant surprise," she said, but I knew it was all bullshit. I played along with it anyway.

I smiled back. "Can I come in?"

She hesitated before answering me. It was apparent that she didn't think it would be a good idea to do so.

"Trust me, I won't be long," I insisted. I felt by saying that she'd be more inclined to let me into her home. And guess what? It worked.

"Sure, come on in," she finally agreed.

I walked inside her place and took in everything in the immediate area of the foyer. The walls were painted white; the floors were hardwood, and it was the expensive kind. I could see the crown molding as I made my way down the hall, and when I entered the grand living room, my breath was taken away by the open floor plan and interior lighting. Even the furniture was immaculate. There was definitely no expense spared.

"Beautiful place you have here," I complimented.

"Thank you. Have a seat," she insisted.

I saw a painting of her father on the wall. It was a sure sign that she was proud of him. "Nice painting of your father," I added.

She looked back at the painting and smiled. "Yeah, my brother had it done for me not too long after my father died. An artist named Fendi did it."

"You mean the designer?"

Alayna chuckled. "No, this guy is local."

"Is your husband here?"

"No, he's at work."

"He's a gym teacher, right?"

"Yeah."

"So, how is that you guys can afford a place like this?" I wondered aloud. I figured that either my husband was financing this, because she was his mistress, or she was in on this insurance fraud stuff too.

"I beg your pardon?" she replied nervously.

"I just want to know if my husband paid for this, or were you in on the insurance fraud too?" I finally came out and said what was on my mind. I was tired of playing the nice guy. "Because if I can remember correctly, you were part-time, so your checks couldn't be that much."

"For your information, my father left me a substantial amount of money when he died. My brother and I also sold his home and kept the proceeds from that, if that's any of your business. And that alone is how I paid for this home I'm living in." She made it a point to explain all of that to me.

I could tell that I hit a nerve, so I wasn't about to stop. "Alayna, tell me why you started sleeping with my husband. And before you start lying, I saw the birthday card you gave him on his thirty-ninth birthday. I read the note you put inside describing how you guys were going to spend that night together. I know you loved him. And I know that you would've left your husband, Levi, for Tim. So, tell me, why smile in my face all these years knowing that you were screwing my husband behind my back?"

"It wasn't like I came on to him," she replied mindlessly. Then she covered her mouth with her hand as she shook her head. I could tell that she immediately regretted the words as soon as they left her mouth.

"Did Levi know about the affair?" I wanted to know.

"Yes," she said.

But the way in which she answered, I knew she was lying.

"When did you tell him?"

"He found out around the time you did."

"And what did he say?"

"He didn't say much. But he didn't want to confront Tim about it."

"So I take it that those two never had the chance to do that?"

Alayna nodded.

"So, what happened the other night?" I got straight to the point. I wanted to hear her version of what happened the night that my husband was murdered.

But at that very moment, she became cold. Stale-faced. No expression whatsoever. "At the advisement of my attorney, I was told not to speak to anyone about that night."

"But you told the cops, right?" I pressed her.

"Yes, but right after that, my attorney told me not to talk to anyone else."

"Are you hiding something?"

"Of course not."

I grew angry and shot up from the chair. "Then tell me what happened?"

"I'm afraid that I'm going to have to tell you to leave." She stood up behind me.

"I'm not going anywhere until you tell me what happened to my husband," I demanded as my pitch got a tad bit higher.

"I'm not telling you shit! Now get out of my house before I make you leave," Alayna threatened.

"And how do you propose to do that?" I dared her. I wanted to hear her tell me what plans she had to put her hands on me so that I could give her an old-fashioned butt whooping. After all the pain she caused my family, I would be glad to put my hands on her and make her suffer like we were.

"Kirsten, don't play with me. I will put you out of my house if you don't leave willingly."

She provoked me. "I would like to see you do that."

She appeared to want to rush me, but then she picked up her cell phone from the coffee table and threatened to call 911.

"Call 'em," I encouraged her. "And tell them why I am here. Let them know that I came here to find out the truth. Find out why you lured my husband out to that salvage yard at that time of the night . . ."

"I didn't lure him anywhere. It was his idea," she blurted out.

"That's not what I heard. Jesse said that it was your idea because you wanted to talk about the affair. Try to get him to take you back."

"Believe anything you want. Jesse doesn't know shit!"

"Oh, trust me, he knows what he's talking about . . ."

Alayna chuckled. "Oh, he does, huh? Well, did he tell you that my brother and I caught him sucking Tim off in Tim's office the same day you stopped by?"

"What?" I replied, taken aback by her statement. What did she mean by saying Jesse was sucking my husband off?

"You heard me correctly. Jesse was sucking Tim's dick, and Alonzo and I caught them in the act." She gloated with a smirk. It was almost like she got a kick out of throwing it in my face.

"That's a lie. Tim wasn't gay." I refuted her claim.

"He may not have been gay, but he was sure as hell bisexual."

"That's a lie!"

"You can believe or not. But I know what I saw, Jesse serving Tim up really good," she said, smiling.

"You think this is funny, don't you?" I snapped.

"Actually, it's not . . ."

"Well, I'll have you know that I will not allow you to smear my husband's good name like that," I protested.

"Face it, Kirsten, I wasn't the only person Tim was seeing behind your back. Tim was what you would call 'a connoisseur of many things.'"

"I'm not listening to this mess!" I shouted, and stormed off in the direction of the front door.

That bitch had really hit an all-time low. Trying to decimate my husband's good reputation by accusing him of immoral acts. Tim had morals and values, so this person that Alayna was trying to describe was nothing like my husband. She was wrong and I could tell that she was trying to deliberately hurt me.

She started walking down on my heels. "Don't run away from the truth!" she shouted behind me.

"You're the devil, you know that, missy!" I shouted back at her, grabbed the door handle, and snatched the door open.

To my surprise her husband, Levi, was standing at the doorway with his house key in hand. He seemed as shocked to see me as I was to see him.

"Hey there," he spoke. But I couldn't bring myself to speak back. I was too up in arms about the attack I had just experienced from Alayna.

"Is everything all right?" he continued.

"Yeah, everything is fine. She was just leaving." Alayna came from behind and pushed Levi out of the way.

"Did you know that your wife was having an affair with my late husband?" I asked him.

Levi became speechless and that's when I knew that Alayna hadn't told him about her infidelities.

"Leave my house at once," Alayna roared.

"I'm not going anywhere until I tell your husband the truth."

"You're gonna get out of here," she added, and then she pushed me.

The force behind her push made me hit the porch hard. *BOOM!*

"Alayna, what's wrong with you?" Levi shouted at her as he came to my rescue.

WHERE THERE'S SMOKE

Alayna slammed the front door and then I heard it lock. There I was, alone with Levi on the porch, and this gave me the opportunity to tell him everything I knew. She hurt me with the affair she had with my husband, and the lies she was trying to spread about his sexuality, so now it was time for some payback.

As Levi helped me up on my feet, he began to apologize for Alayna's behavior. I immediately told him that this had no reflection on him, but that I needed to talk to him. I persuaded him to escort me to my car. This way I could talk to him without any interference from Alayna. He happily obliged.

As we made our way from his house, I started off by saying, "I apologize for the intrusion. I see you just came home, so I'm sure you wanted to go inside and take a load off and relax a little bit."

"I'm actually on lunch right now, so I'm good."

"Well, I'm sure you heard about my husband?"

"Yeah, I did, and I also heard about the affair that my wife was having with him."

"And you were okay with it?"

"Actually, I wasn't. As a matter of fact, I kind of suspected that something was going on, but every time I confronted Alayna about it, she kept denying it. But the truth finally came out the other day when the FBI stopped over here and told me while they were confronting her about your husband's murder. The whole thing was a shit show."

"I can imagine."

"So, how did you find out?" he asked.

"I actually caught them in the act the other day."

"Oh, really?"

"Yes, I stopped by the station to see Tim, but when I tried to get in the office, the door was locked. And when he finally opened it, I saw Alayna and him looking very suspicious. Their behavior was off."

"Did you confront him at that moment?"

"As a matter of fact, I did. But they denied it. I left there in an uproar because I knew something wasn't right. You know women, we have that intuition. And nine times out of ten, we are always right."

"What made you stop by here today?"

"To confront Alayna. Ask her what happened the night my husband was killed."

"And what did she say?"

"She didn't say anything. She gave me some old bogus excuse about how her attorney told her not to talk to anyone."

"What attorney? She doesn't have one."

"I don't care if she has one or not. But I do care about the fact that she's hiding something."

"What do you think she's hiding?"

"I don't know. But I talked to one of the firefighters down at the station and he believed that Alayna had something to do with Tim's murder."

Levi chuckled in disbelief. "No way! Alayna is many things. But a killer? No way possible."

"The guy said that Tim broke it off with her and she took it hard. And that meeting was her idea. She lured him out there and gave him an ultimatum, and when he declined to take her back, she had him killed."

Levi started shaking his head, as if what I was saying was unfathomable. But I started drilling it in his head. "I know that you don't believe this, but it's true. Your wife had a sick fixation that if she couldn't have him, no one else could."

"Nah, I don't believe that. Not Alayna. Now the cheating part, I believe. But she doesn't have a malicious bone in her body."

"Well, if you know your wife so well, did you know that she's been seeing my husband for a couple of years now? When I was cleaning out his office, I found a birthday card she gave him on his thirty-ninth birthday. I know that very night they had sex at the station."

Levi cringed at my admission. "Look, I've heard enough. I'm gonna say goodbye for now, so I can go inside and talk to my wife," he said.

"Good luck with that," I told him, and then I got into my car. And when I looked out of my driver's-side window and saw him walking at a fast pace toward his house, I couldn't let the chance slip away without shouting a warning at him.

As soon as the window was halfway down, I shouted, "You may want to get her an attorney, because as soon as the detectives figure out that she set my husband up, she's going to prison for a long time!"

He turned around and responded, "I'm sorry, but you got the wrong person."

"Yeah, right," I chuckled, and then I drove away.

CHAPTER 13

Alayna

LEVI CAME INTO THE HOUSE CALMLY AND CLOSED THE FRONT DOOR. I couldn't see him from where I was sitting in the living room, but I knew that I would see him in less than five seconds flat. I could feel the tension brewing in the air, and I knew I was going to have some explaining to do because the questions were coming.

"Did you love him?" he asked as soon as he got within arm's reach of me.

I pretended to be looking at the television when he walked into the living room. But if he'd asked, I couldn't tell him what movie was playing or what it was about.

"Love who?" I replied, also pretending not to know who he was talking about.

"Tim, Alayna. Tim."

"Why would you ask me that?"

"Stop avoiding the question and answer it."

"You want to know the truth?" I asked him, giving him the choice to decide if he wanted his feelings hurt or not.

"Yes, the truth."

"Okay, then yes, I did love him," I finally answered.

Levi's face suddenly looked defeated. It looked like a bunch of air was sucked out of him at that very moment. He stood there and combed his fingers through what little bit of hair he had on his head.

"Why didn't you tell me this before?"

"Because I knew that you wouldn't have been able to handle it," I told him nonchalantly. I mean, at this point, I was twiddling my fingers about this whole thing with him. So trying to preserve his feelings went out the door a long time ago.

"So that's your answer?"

"That's the only one I have."

"Why are you acting like you don't fucking care?"

"Because I don't, Levi. I'm done with this marriage. For these last few days, you've demonstrated to me that you care more about everyone else than me. I mean, how dare you let the FBI agents into my home without my permission? You just let them walk all in my house that *I* paid for and interrogate me like we're in an interrogation room? This is my sanctuary. Not somewhere where they can walk all through here like they pay bills. But you didn't care. All you thought about was your own ass. You were so scared that they'd try to implicate you in my brother's case that you'd let them do anything they want."

"That's not true!"

"Yes, it is, Levi. You're a fucking sellout and you know it. And that's why I want a divorce!" I boomed. I was giving him my undivided attention now.

Hurt appeared in his eyes. "So you're saying you want out of this marriage?" He seemed to be confused.

"Yup, I want out. You can go back and live with your mama, and I will stay here."

"I'm not leaving here."

"Yes, you are." I stood up.

"No, I'm not. This is as much my place as it is yours."

"But I purchased this house with my father's money. So you have no claims to it."

KIKI SWINSON

"Like hell I don't."

"So, whatcha gonna do? Take me to court for it? Levi, I swear, I would bury you if you tried to take this place from me."

"Like you did Tim? You're gonna have me killed too?"

"Fuck you, Levi! Get out of my house!"

Levi gawked at me. "Tell me the truth!" he demanded as he began to walk toward me.

"Don't come near me, Levi," I warned him, and turned to walk in the opposite direction.

While I was walking to our bedroom, his cell phone started ringing. He stopped walking and answered it.

"Hello," I heard him say. "Hey, Mama, can I call you back?"

And that's when I turned around, because I was going to get in that conversation.

"No, don't call her back. Pack your clothes and take them to her house!" I shouted. And I shouted loud enough for her to hear me.

I couldn't hear what she said, but when Levi was trying to downplay what I was saying, I interjected again. "Don't believe anything he's telling you. I told him I wanted a divorce and for him to leave my house at this very moment!" I shouted once more.

"Hold on," Levi said into the phone, and at that point he put the call on speaker so that I could hear her voice. "She can hear you now," he continued.

"Alayna, can you hear me?" his mother started off.

"Yes, I can," I acknowledged, and sighed heavily.

"Well, good, then, because I am only going to say this once . . ." she stated, and then she paused. "I don't know what you got going on in that mind of yours, but you're not going to inflict heartache and pain on my son. Levi has been nothing but good to you. And my entire family has been good to you, so you better watch yourself, young lady, because God don't like ugly!" she added.

76

"Are you done?" I asked her.

"Yes, I'm done."

"Good, because I'm only going to say this once. I've put up with a lot of your son's shit, your shit, and your family's shit, and now it's time for me to throw in the towel."

"Don't talk to my mother like that!" Levi interjected.

"Shut the fuck up! I'll talk to her the way I want. She asked for this and I'm going to give it to her," I scolded him, and then I turned my attention back to the phone he was holding in his hand. "Now, like I was saying, I told your son I wanted a divorce. So he needs to pack up his shit and get out. I don't want to go to counseling, and I don't want to fix it. I want to move on. So, can you talk to him and get it through his head that what we have is dead?"

"You mean like that man you were with the other night when he got shot?" Levi's mother commented.

"You don't know shit, old lady!" I barked. "Now just tell your son to pack his shit and get out of my house!" I screeched, and then I stormed into the bathroom and slammed the door.

I heard Levi say a few more words to his mother and then he ended the call. I thought he was going to try to talk to me through the bathroom door, but he didn't. Instead, I heard him in the bedroom rambling around. I figured he was in there gathering his things, so I stayed in the bathroom until I heard him walk out the front door and close it behind himself.

I waited an additional ten minutes before I walked out of the bathroom, just to make sure that he was gone. When I finally entered into the bedroom and saw that he took a lot of his clothes, I felt a sense of relief he got the picture that our relationship had run its course and I wanted it to be over. I decided that while he was away, I would pack up the rest of his things. This way he could just come and pick it up and leave. The less time he spent here, the better.

CHAPTER 14

Alonzo

Normally, my phone calls with Pricilla be chill, but this particular conversation was cringeworthy. All she wanted to talk about the entire call was the wedding. I wanted to say fuck the wedding. I am in fucking jail fighting for my life and all she can think about is the wedding? I mean, did she not know that I was locked up for three counts of murder?

"Listen, I know you're excited about the wedding, but I don't want to talk about it every time I call."

"Whatcha want to talk about? Your murder charges? Because that shit is depressing."

"No, I don't, but I'm sure there's something else we can talk about," I pointed out.

"So, whatcha don't wanna get married now?"

"Pricilla, who said that I didn't want to get married?"

"It's your words and your actions."

"Honey, I am in jail. How can I think about something like that at a time like this?" I expressed to her.

"Well, why didn't you just say that?"

"Why do I have to, Pricilla? I am going through it in here. And

78

now that Tim is dead, that's some more shit added to my plate. So, how can I think about wedding stuff right now?" I explained.

Pricilla sucked her teeth. "Yeah, whatever," she commented.

"Where is your mama? I haven't heard her mouth since we've been on the phone."

"She went home."

"Thank God! At one point I didn't think she had a home to go to."

"Stop it, Zo. Don't try to change the subject."

"I'm not trying to change the subject. But tell me why was she giving my sister problems the other day? Questioning her about Tim's murder and shit. She needs to mind her fucking business!"

"Oh, so Alayna ran back and told you what happened?"

"Yeah, she told me. Is that a problem?"

"Well, she acted like it wasn't a problem when she and my mom were having that conversation."

"Well, she did."

"Well, did she tell you that I took up for her when my mama kept giving her shit?"

"No, she didn't."

"Well, she should've told you, because I had her back. I guess that explains why she hasn't been over here."

"Can you blame her? If you're being accused of something, would you go back to that place?"

"No."

"Exactly. So stop acting dumb!"

"I'm not acting dumb, Zo! So don't talk to me like that!" she yelled.

"Look, I didn't mean that. I'm sorry!"

"Don't talk to me like that ever again, Zo!"

I sighed heavily. "Yeah, yeah, yeah!" I said, and a couple of seconds later, the timer on the call started sounding off.

"You have one minute left," the pre-recorded message announced. And, boy, was that like music to my ears!

"Are you calling me back?" she asked.

"Nah, I'm going to go and lay down. I'll call you back later," I told her. But in reality I wasn't calling her complaining ass back. She'd be lucky if she heard from me in the next couple of days. After that headache she just gave me, I was going to have to ask the nurse lady for some aspirin when she came around tonight.

"I love you," she said.

"Yeah, I love you too," I replied nonchalantly before the phone hung up. I placed the receiver on the hook and disconnected the call myself. I'd never done that before. But today it was warranted.

When I was back in my cell, I laid down on my bunk. My cellmate was already sitting on his bed drawing a cartoon character on his sketch pad. The little dude was nice with the pencil. "You almost done with that?" I asked him.

"Yeah, it's almost finished," he replied.

"Which character is that?" My questions continued as I situated myself to lie comfortably on my back.

"This nigga I made up named Hero Dan. He's the weed man that got that superpower shit, that gives you powers to fly and kick down metal doors and shit."

I chuckled. Wayne was funny as hell. The little dude was a real-live comedian on the low. He was a very immature guy, but he kept me sane in this place. "Does he grow it, or does he have a supplier?" I joked.

"He's the grower."

I laughed even more as I pictured my cellmate's superhero growing weed that gives regular niggas superpowers. I could definitely use some of that right now. See if it'll help me break out of this bitch and fly away to never-never land.

"Why don't you start a comic book?"

"Yeah, I thought about it. But that shit takes too much time to do."

"You act like you're getting out of here tomorrow."

"Shiid . . . you never know. Niggas is getting out of jail every day because of overcrowding and that Covid shit."

"But you haven't even went to trial yet for your charges, so you got time," I reminded him, and then I kicked up underneath the bottom of his book with my feet.

"Damn, nigga, you almost made me mess up this nigga's arms," Wayne complained.

"It isn't the end of the world," I commented, and then my mind drifted off. I started thinking about how I couldn't believe that Tim was no longer among the living. The dude was literally dead. And my sister had the motherfucker killed all behind me. I also couldn't help but think about why she used K-Rock and his homeboy to kill Tim. Now I know that they're legit street dudes, but they do sloppy work. I could only hope those guys didn't jam her up if the cops found out that they pulled the trigger and came looking for them.

On another note, though, thinking about how Tim was going to sell me out, to save his own ass, justified his death. If I were on the streets, I would've killed him myself because there was no way that I would've been able to allow him to roam around freely like that, without consequences. It's not in my nature. As far as I was concerned, he created his own demise. Fucking rat!

As I lay there running everything through my mind, I wondered how my little sister was doing at this very moment. I wondered if she was at home arguing with her dumb-ass husband or were the homicide detectives out there harassing her, and shit. Either way I knew that I needed to call and check up on her. So I hopped out of bed and grabbed the first phone I could get my hands on. I dialed her number the first time and let it ring five times until her cell phone recording picked up and then I disconnected the call. I waited for a minute and then I called right back. This time it only rang twice before she answered. Hearing her voice was like a sigh of relief.

So, after listening to the jail recording, Alayna pressed the option button 5 and then she said, "What's up, bro?"

I lit up like a Christmas tree. "Where were you the first time I called? You had me worried there for a bit."

"I was in the bathroom."

"Where you at?"

"Home."

"Is Levi there?"

"Hell no. I put his ass out the other day. I believe he's at his mother's house."

"Why did you put him out?"

"I told you that I was divorcing him, Zo. I wasn't pulling your leg when I first told you that."

"What did he say when you told him that you were divorcing him?"

"Well, he didn't believe me at first. But after I drilled it in his head a few times, he got the message."

"So, what have you been doing since I last seen you?"

"Nothing much. Just been taking it easy. Cleaned up the house and ran a few errands."

"I talked to Pricilla earlier and told her that I didn't appreciate the way her mother talked to you the other day."

"And what did she say?"

"She said that she took your side and told her mama to leave you alone."

"Yeah, she did. But believe me, she could've done more."

"Yeah, I know." I agreed because I knew how Pricilla operated. She did the bare minimum for everyone except herself. "So, other than that, you're good?"

"Well, besides the homicide detectives who are investigating

Tim's murder and who stopped by and left their business card on the front door, it's been pretty quiet."

"When did they stop by?"

"Earlier today. But I wasn't here. They left their card in the crack of my front door. And there was a message written on the back for me to call 'em."

"Are you going to call 'em?"

"Not until I lawyer up."

"Smart girl. Because you know that if you go down there alone, they're gonna try to railroad your ass. See, I knew there was a reason why I had to call you. You've been on my mind really heavy all day."

"Who do you think I should call?"

"Call my attorney and tell him the situation and then ask him to refer you to someone. Maybe someone in his firm?"

"Yeah, good idea."

"How do you feel right now?" I had to ask. I was becoming extremely worried about her.

"Under the circumstances, I'm okay. Can't wait for you to come home and all of this shit blows over. And speaking of shit, I forgot to tell you that Jesse brought his ass over here to confront me about the night that Tim got shot."

"When was this?"

"A couple of days ago."

"Damn, I wished I was there because I would've bitch slapped his ass. But I'm sure you handled his ass."

"I did. But that's not it, guess who else stopped by?"

"Who?"

"Tim's wife, and she was talking shit to me too. I was like, who's gonna bring their asses by here next?"

"What did she say?"

"She wanted receipts. Basically, asking how long I had been seeing Tim and had he paid for everything in my house, being that I was his mistress?"

"No fucking way! She got some balls!" I chuckled loudly because I knew the deal. Not only had my father's money helped purchase Alayna's place and the high-end finishes inside, I also helped fund her lifestyle with my insurance fraud money. But whoever was listening on this recorded line didn't need to know that.

"You know she told Levi about the affair?"

Shocked by her statement, I said, "He was there?"

"He came at the tail end, but he was there long enough for her to tell him everything."

"And what did he say to you?"

"Well, he started off trying to question me, but I shut him down and told him I wanted a divorce, and immediately after that is when I told him to leave my house."

"Damn, Alayna, you're gangster as shit!"

"You have to be when you're fucking with morons like the people I've been dealing with lately."

"You know that if I was home, none of this shit would be going on. Especially that stunt Jesse pulled. He knew he wouldn't have been able to get away with that if I was home."

"Of course, I know that, and he knew it too. That's how he was able to get up the balls to stop by."

"Have you spoken to Paul or Mike since all of this stuff went down?"

"I only talked to them that one time when I went by there after you got arrested, and that was the time I ran into Tim too. But other than that, no."

"That's fucked up that they hadn't tried to reach out to you. I hope they aren't on that sucker shit!"

"There's no telling with those guys."

"Yeah, tell me about it," I agreed, and then I changed the subject. "You know, I don't want to get married anymore."

Shocked by my admission, Alayna responded, "Really?"

"Yeah, Pricilla has taken the fun out of it. I mean, every time we get on the phone, she wants to discuss who she added to the guest list and then starts talking about what she wants to add to the menu and how she may have to make the decision about the cake without me. Does she realize that I am locked up, and talking about wedding shit is the last thing on my mind?"

Alayna chuckled. "Did you tell her that?"

"I didn't tell her that I didn't want to get married anymore, but I expressed to her that right now ain't the time to talk about it. I've got other important shit on my mind. Like getting out of here, for one."

"So, are you saying that you don't want to get married *now* because you're in your feelings? Or is this a decision you've thought about wholeheartedly?"

"Both."

"Wait, so you're saying you're not getting married anymore at all?"

"Yup, it's final. I am no longer getting married."

"Oh, shit! When Pricilla finds this out, she's gonna hit the fan," she warned me.

"Yeah, I know. So I may have to move into your crib when I get out of here," I joked.

"You know, *mi casa es su casa.*"

"I appreciate that," I told her, and then the one-minute pre-recorded message chimed in.

"Damn, that was fast," I commented.

"Yeah, it was," Alayna agreed.

"So, what are you getting ready to get into?" I wanted to know.

"I'm gonna stay in the house and watch a few movies. But in the morning I'm gonna call your attorney and see what he says about my situation."

"Yeah, you do that, and I'll call you tomorrow evening."

"Okay. I love you."

"I love you too, sis. Be careful out there."

"I will," she assured me, and then our call ended.

Feeling better that I touched base with my sister, I headed back into my cell and lay back down. This time I was able to rest knowing that she was in the house safe. It did, however, alarm me that the cops wanted her to come down to the precinct to talk to them. I knew from experience that they weren't going to stop fucking with her until she did go to see them. But she better have a good lawyer in tow.

CHAPTER 15

Kirsten

I WAS GOING THROUGH TIM'S CLOTHES, DECIDING WHAT SUIT TO bury him in, when I heard a knock on the front door. My parents had taken the kids out to get dinner so that I could have this time alone, but that now went out the window. I wondered who could be on the other side of my front door, but once I was within two feet of it, I verbalized my thoughts.

"Who is it?" I called out.

"It's Detective Showers and Pittman," I heard one voice say.

After identifying who was at the door, I opened it and greeted both men. "How can I help you gentlemen this evening?"

"May we come in?" Detective Showers asked.

"Sure," I said, and allowed them both to enter my home. I escorted them to the living-room sofa and offered them something to drink. After they declined, I asked what brought them by.

"We came to check on you. See if you heard anything since we last talked?" Detective Showers asked as he and the other detective took a seat on the sofa.

I sat down across from them. "I was hoping that you guys were coming here to give me an update."

"We're still conducting interviews and gathering information," Detective Showers said.

"Yeah, and we're waiting on forensic results to come back from the lab too," Detective Pittman chimed in.

"What information have you gathered?" I wanted to know.

"Since the investigation is still active, I'm afraid we can't discuss our findings with you at this moment," Detective Showers continued.

"The person who can lead you to the killers is less than fifteen minutes away from here," I pointed out.

"We've reached back out to her, so we're just waiting on her to get back in touch with us," Detective Showers added.

"Have you been to her house?"

"Yes, as a matter of fact, we stopped by there this morning. No one was there, so I left my business card in her door," he said.

"Are you guys looking at her as a suspect?"

"Again, since this case is still active, we cannot discuss any of the specifics at this moment." Detective Showers wouldn't let up any info.

I sighed heavily out of frustration. "I paid her a visit the other day," I volunteered.

At the mention of my visit to Alayna, both detectives sat straight up. "What did you two talk about?" Detective Pittman wanted to know.

"I asked her what happened the night my husband was killed," I replied.

"And what did she say?" Detective Pittman pressed me.

"She told me that her attorney advised her not to talk to anyone until we're in court."

Both detectives looked at one another. Detective Showers chuckled. "Is that so?"

"That explains why she hasn't called us back," Detective Pittman interjected.

"So, does that mean that she's off the hook from talking to you guys?"

"Oh, of course not. It just means that when we do talk to her again, she's going to have her attorney present."

"Yeah, and that also means that she's got something to hide."

"Unfortunately, Mrs. Stancil, that's what people do when they have something to hide. They lawyer up," Detective Showers agreed.

"So, what happens now?"

"We wait for her lawyer's call and then we go from there," Detective Pittman stated.

"And that could take forever."

"If we don't hear from her in another day or so, then we will put pressure on her. Don't worry. But let me switch gears a little, do you think there could be a link from the murder victims of Alonzo Riddick to your husband's murder?" Detective Showers chimed back in.

"What do you mean by that?" I asked.

"Do you think someone sought retribution against Tim for the victims that were murdered in Alonzo's case?" he clarified.

Appalled by their question, I rolled my eyes at the detective. "What kind of question is that? No one sought retribution against my husband behind the murdered victims who died at the hands of Alonzo. My husband had nothing to do with those people getting killed. The person who killed my husband was right there when he was gunned down. But you let her go and now you can't get ahold of her," I spat. I was pissed and offended by his questions.

"Oh, we will, don't you worry," Detective Showers assured me.

The detectives and I spoke for a few more minutes and then I grew tired of their conversation. I told them I had to get back to what I was doing before they arrived. They thanked me for my time and left.

Still angry by the entire conversation, I went back to my bedroom to lie down. I was too drained mentally to continue on with finding my husband something to be buried in. I figured I'd deal with it later tonight after I cleared my head.

CHAPTER 16

Alonzo

"*R*IDDICK, GET READY! YOU'VE GOT AN ATTORNEY VISIT," THE CO yelled from the hallway of the cell block.

I was lying in my bed when the CO shouted my name, so I jumped up from my bunk, slipped on my shoes, and exited my cell, all the while wondering what kind of shit my lawyer was going to lay down on me today. I hoped that it was good news, because I really needed some of that right now. But it wouldn't surprise me to hear him ask me questions about Tim's murder, since I hadn't heard anything from the cops investigating that case. Alayna warned me that they'd probably be paying me a visit sometime soon, but as of yet, they hadn't reared their ugly faces.

"Open cell block 8-B," the CO radioed the command pod. Seconds later, the door slid open. I stepped into the small cage, like a routine, and watched as the first door closed. Immediately the second cell door on the opposite side of me opened, and that allowed me to step into the hallway.

"Turn toward the wall," the CO instructed me. So I turned and faced the wall and that's when he handcuffed my wrists behind my back. After that, he led me out of the cell block and into a nearby corridor. It only took us two minutes to get to the attorney and inmate visiting room.

When the CO opened the door and escorted me inside, I wasn't at all surprised to see two plainclothes cops sitting down at the table opposite me.

"Alonzo Riddick," one of the guys said as the CO started uncuffing me.

"Yeah," I answered after the CO pulled the seat out for me to sit down.

"Y'all good?" the CO asked both cops after I sat down in the chair.

"Yes, we can take it from here," the same cop replied.

The CO exited the room while I was sizing both men up.

"Mr. Riddick, I'm Detective Showers, and this is my partner, Detective Pittman. We're investigating the murder of Tim Stancil—"

"And what does that have to do with me?" I didn't hesitate to ask him.

"Well, I'm sure you know that your sister was there when he was murdered?" he replied.

"I heard something like that," I said casually.

"Have you spoken with her about it?" His questions continued.

"When she came to visit me last, she didn't want to talk about it," I lied.

My plan was to make the cops believe I knew nothing because Alayna wouldn't tell me anything. This would eliminate any chance for them to use me to testify against my sister at a grand jury indictment hearing.

"Why didn't she want to talk about it?" he pressed me.

"She just said that it hurts to think about what happened. And that she didn't want to rehash it. That's it. So I left it alone."

"Who told you that she was there?" the same detective wanted to know.

"One night I called my house, and she and my fiancée told me."

"Do you remember when that was?" he probed.

I knew what he was doing. The calls in this jail were monitored, so I knew he already knew the answer to that question. But I was gonna play the game and give him what he wanted. "I think it was the day after the murder."

"Did she sound devastated or distraught?"

"She sounded like she was both. I could definitely tell that she was hurting."

"Can you tell me why?" the cop asked. He wouldn't let up.

"I hate to say it, but she loved him."

"Did you know about the relationship they were having?"

"Not until after the fact," I responded nonchalantly.

"So, do you think she's capable of murder?"

Taken aback by his question, I burst into laughter. "My sister? Murder? Come on now, sir. Not Alayna. She's a sweetheart. She wouldn't hurt a fly," I told him.

"Do you think that she's capable of having him killed?" the same cop came back. I knew he was trying to get a reaction out of me, and I wasn't going to feed into it.

"Who would she get to kill him? She knows no one," I answered candidly.

"I didn't ask you who would she get to do it. I asked you if she's capable of hiring someone to do the job for her?"

"No, she's not capable of doing that. It would take someone with a cold and cruel heart to have someone killed. And didn't I mention that she loved him?" I reiterated.

"There are people who kill people they love all the time," Detective Showers pointed out.

"Not my sister, though. She's a different breed."

"What about you?"

"What about me?"

"Are you a different breed?"

"I don't understand the question."

"Did you kill those people?"

I abruptly stood up from my seat. "Look, man, I didn't come in here to answer questions about me," I stated. "Hey, CO, I'm done!" I shouted.

"Wait, hold up, calm down." The other detective stood up and leveled his arms, suggesting for me to sit back down. But I stood there.

"I'm calm," I assured him.

"Well, have a seat then," he instructed me.

"For what? I'm done here," I replied. "Hey, CO, I'm done here!" I shouted once more.

"Listen, Riddick, let's face it. We know that your sister was involved some way in Tim's murder. We just haven't figured out what it was. And we got a hunch that it could've had something to do with your case, seeing as though he was cooperating with the federal agents in your insurance fraud case. It seems as though he could've helped put you away for a long time."

I chuckled. "That sounds pretty good. Too bad it's all a theory," and as I concluded my comment, the CO was walking into the visiting room.

"You ready?" he asked me.

"Yeah, I'm ready," I told him, and placed my arms behind my back so that he could cuff my wrists. I kept my eyes on the detectives the entire time. "Thanks for the visit, you guys. Ain't nothing like getting out of that little-ass cell they put you in when you're in a place like this," I added.

"Don't mention it," Detective Showers replied. "But the way things seem to look for you, you might be living in that little-ass cell for the rest of your life," he added with a grimace.

"Yeah, Showers, you might be right," his partner agreed.

I smiled. "Says who?" I replied, and then I turned around to leave. "Good day, gentlemen." I concluded my conversation with them while I was being escorted from the room.

On the way back to the cell block, I couldn't help but wonder what kind of evidence they had on Alayna and whether they were close to arresting her. Damn, I hoped they were just here fishing for information. Because if they had anything to pin Tim's murder on her, then she was fucked. She had to get an attorney ASAP.

CHAPTER 17

Alayna

AFTER SPEAKING WITH ALONZO'S ATTORNEY, HE REFERRED ME TO his colleague Albert Rosenberg. So I was here at the law firm, waiting in the lobby for my four o'clock appointment. The waiting area was empty, of course, except for this one guy waiting to see someone. He looked like a low-level drug dealer. If I could guess, he'd probably got busted with a couple pounds of weed. Or maybe he needed representation because his trap house was busted, and they found an ounce of crack cocaine? Whatever it was, it couldn't be much, because his thin gold chain, fake gold watch, and beat-up Jordan sneakers told it all.

I saw him look at me a few times, hoping to get my attention, but I refused to give eye contact to this joker. The last thing I wanted to do was make him think that I was interested in him. But that didn't do any good because as much as I avoided eye contact with this fool, he got up the nerve to say hello to me. I pretended not to hear him, so he said hello again. This time he said it louder. "Hello, pretty lady."

I was two seconds from ripping him a new asshole, but I contained my composure and kept it ladylike. I turned around slowly and replied, "Hello."

"What's your name?"

"Alayna," I said reluctantly.

"That's a beautiful name."

"Thank you."

"You're welcome. My name is Greg."

"Nice to meet you, Greg."

"Same here. So, do you have a man?"

"I'm actually married," I boldly said. I even said it with pride—anything that would keep this has-been from thinking that he'd have a chance in hell with me.

"Happily?" he pressed.

"Absolutely. He's the love of my life," I lied. If only he knew that I hated Levi's guts, and that we were on our way to divorce court. He wouldn't believe it from my actions.

"He's a lucky man."

I smiled. "I'll remind him of that when I get home." I lied once more. I mean, I was pouring it on thick. "So, who are you here to see?" I changed the subject. I was more curious to see who his attorney was and what he was here for, if he'd volunteer that information.

"Rosenberg," he said.

"Oh, really? Me too."

"Oh, cool."

"So, does he represent you?"

"Yes, I got a DUI and I hired him to keep me out of jail, being that this was my second offense," he answered.

And what do you know? I was wrong. Here I thought he was here for drug charges and homeboy is a fucking alcoholic.

"So he does traffic cases too?"

"Well, I was actually charged with vehicular homicide too," he added.

Boy, was I stunned to hear that, and my mouth dropped wide open. "No way! Really?"

"Yeah, see, I was coming from a party after having a few drinks and this guy was riding a bike without reflectors down a dark road and got in my way and I ran him over."

"Oh, my God! Did he die on the spot?"

"No, he did a few days later in the hospital."

"Wait, where did this happen?"

"In Norfolk, about a year ago."

"Oh, yeah, I remember hearing about that. So you're just now going to court for it?"

"Yeah, it takes a long time for a homicide case to go before a judge."

"Think you're going to beat it?"

"No, there's no chance that I'm going to beat it. But I am trying to get the charges reduced so that if convicted, I could get lesser time."

"So, what is the victim's family saying?"

"Oh, they've been down my ass. They've been trying to get the prosecutor to convince the judge to give me life in prison."

"How old are you?"

"Twenty-nine."

"Damn! You're young."

"Yeah, I know."

"Do you have any kids?"

"Yeah, I have two sons."

"How old?"

"Five and two."

"Ah, man, they're young."

"I know. So let's pray that the judge has leniency on me because it would tear me up inside if I can't see my boys grow up."

"I'm sure it would. But don't worry, you'll be fine."

"Thanks, I appreciate that."

"So, what time is your appointment with Rosenberg?" I asked, wanting to know if he was going to go in the guy's office before me.

"It was at three, but I got here late. So he told me that I'll be his last appointment for the day."

"Mrs. Curry, Mr. Rosenberg will see you now," the receptionist announced.

I stood up from my chair when I heard my name. "Nice meeting you. And good luck!" I said to Greg, and then I followed the receptionist into the attorney's office. Immediately after I walked across the threshold, the receptionist introduced me to Mr. Rosenberg, a bald, white, medium-build guy. Well groomed too. He kind of put me in mind of the white actor Stanley Tucci.

"Nice to meet you, Mrs. Curry, come on in," he insisted as he greeted me after he stood up from his desk and extended a handshake.

"Nice to meet you too," I said. After we released each other's hand, I sat down in the chair placed in front of his desk.

"So, what brings you by?" he wanted to know.

"Well, as you already know, I was referred by my brother's attorney, Swartz . . ."

"Oh, yeah, your brother is the firefighter accused of the triple homicide."

"Yeah, so the other night I was with another firefighter, who was murdered in Chesapeake at that salvage junkyard . . ."

"I heard about that."

"Well, I spoke with the homicide detectives on the night it happened, but now they want to talk to me again. So I was told that I needed to seek counsel before I sit down and do another interview with them."

"Did you murder the victim?"

"No."

"Do you know who did?"

"No."

"Okay, so we're off to a great start," he said as he pulled out a pen and started scribbling words down on a legal pad.

"What was the victim's name?"

"Tim Stancil."

"And who was he to you?"

"He was my boss and chief firefighter at the Haygood Fire Station in Virginia Beach. We were also seeing each other."

"What do you mean you were 'seeing' him?"

"We were having an affair."

"So you're both married?"

"Yes."

"Okay, so tell me your account of what happened the night the victim was murdered."

"Well, we had broken up earlier that day, so I called him and told him that we needed to discuss what happened and I agreed to meet at the salvage junkyard place. While we were out there talking, two guys pop up out of nowhere. They cornered him and I tried to run. But one of the guys aimed his gun at me, stopped me, and said that if I ran, he was going to kill the both of us. So I stood still and watched them as they robbed him."

"Did he resist?"

"In the beginning, yes."

"What did he say?"

"He was telling them that he wasn't giving them shit. And that's when the guys started talking shit back to him. One of them put the barrel of their gun to his head and threatened to pull the trigger if he didn't give up his money. So I started yelling at Tim to give them what they wanted. But he wouldn't listen and decided to play hero by trying to take the gun from one of the guys. They were struggling for the gun and then I heard a gunshot. Seconds later, Tim fell to the ground and the guys ran off."

"Did they ever take anything from you?"

"No, but believe me, they wanted to. Tim stopped them from doing it because of what transpired with him."

"Did you try to help Tim up from the ground after he was shot?"

"No, I was too scared."

"Then what did you do?"

"I hopped inside my Jeep and locked the door."

"At any point, Alayna, did you just leave him lying there?" Rosenberg wanted to know.

"What do you mean?"

"Did you leave the scene?"

"No, but I locked myself up in my Jeep and called 911."

"So you stayed there until help came?"

"Yes."

"When did you realize the victim was dead?"

"While I was talking to the 911 dispatcher on the phone."

"So you got back out of your car?"

"Yes."

"Did the 911 dispatcher instruct you to get back out of your car to check on the victim?"

"Yes, she did. But I waited a few minutes before I did it."

"Why?"

"I had to make sure that the people responsible for his death were gone first."

"Understood," he said as he continued to write down most of what I was saying. "So, did anyone take a gun residue test on you while you were at the scene?"

"Yes, they did."

"Do you remember the names of the homicide detectives?"

"Yes, it was Detective Showers and Detective Pittman."

"I've heard of Showers. Not so sure of the other guy."

"I hope not anything bad."

"No," he said as he wrote something else down. "Do you remember how long they kept you out there?"

"Long enough to ask me a ton of questions."

"At any time at all, did they say you were free to leave?"

"Not until they were done with questioning me."

"Have you spoken to the detective since?"

"Nope. But they've been by my place, and since I wasn't there, they left me their card with a note written on the back for me to call them back."

"So everything you told me today, you told them the same thing?"

"Yup, every word."

"Okay," he said. Then he picked up his cell phone and started searching through the contents of it. He looked pretty engaged. When he started reading what was before him, and then started texting, that's when I knew it had nothing to do with my case. This was something personal.

"With everything I just told you, do you think those guys are going to try and charge me with Tim's murder?" I spoke.

He looked up from his phone. "Well, at this point it doesn't seem like they have anything on you. But trust me, they're digging and they're hoping that after speaking with you again, they can somehow catch you in a lie. But if you are telling them the truth, then it would be impossible to do so."

"So, do you recommend that I speak to them again?"

"Well, let me put it like this, they aren't going anywhere. This is an active murder investigation and there's a lot of fire being ignited by the mayor to crack down on all of these murders, so they're gonna harass you or anyone else, for that matter, until they find someone to charge. It's not personal, until they make it personal. Now, then, I don't advise you to talk to them alone again. You should have counsel with you every time you speak with those guys, because they aren't your friends. They will pretend to be your friend. Well, actually, one of the detectives will play good cop, while the other one plays the bad cop. You know the shit you see on TV?"

I chuckled. "Yeah, I've seen it."

"So then you know what I am talking about."

"How much would it be to retain you?"

"Well, since you haven't been charged in the victim's murder and only need counsel escort to protect you in police custody, it will be a flat fee of fifteen hundred dollars for up to a two-hour visit. Now if they find evidence somewhere and charge you with the victim's murder, then I charge four hundred dollars an hour and my initial retainer is thirty thousand."

"Oh, wow! That's a lot!" I commented. This motherfucker was more expensive than Zo's lawyer. I was talking to the wrong guy. I needed to see other attorneys and check around for better prices because I would end up in the poor house if I hired this guy to represent me. Now was the time to pray that those cops didn't dig up anything on me to charge me with Tim's murder. If they did, I was fucked.

Rosenberg chuckled. "It's not a lot when you're gambling with your life."

"You're right about that," I agreed.

"Well, we can start off with accompanying you down to the precinct and make sure that you don't answer the wrong questions, and then we go from there. What do you think?"

I thought for a moment and then I said, "So, who's going to set up the interview with the detectives?"

"My secretary will. You wouldn't have to do anything but show up."

"Okay, then, let's do it," I replied with a face of optimism.

He got excited. "Awesome."

"Wait, do you need the detective's business card?" I asked him while sifting through the items inside my purse.

"Yes, that would be helpful," he agreed.

After I found it in the coin pouch of my purse, I handed it to him. He took it and looked at it. He immediately gave me a full rundown on Detective Showers after getting a glimpse of his name and the location of his office at the same time.

"Yes, I know this guy. He's one of those newly appointed, badass detectives looking to make noise out there in Chesapeake. He used to work narcotics a few years ago. Busted a few of my clients on some major drug charges. He even got away with an illegal search with one of my cases and the judge took his word over my client, who, by the way, was a first-time offender. Had no priors."

"No way," I said in disbelief.

"No, really. My client was traveling on the Chinese bus with an ounce of heroin and fentanyl, and that same detective, along with his partner, tricked her into allowing them to search her bag. They told her that someone gave them a description of her and said that she was carrying a lot of drugs into the city. And that if she doesn't cooperate and hand over the drugs, he's going to make sure that she never sees the light of day ever again. So, what do you do in a situation like that? The girl was only nineteen years old. She was freaking terrified to death."

"Wow! He's a monster."

"Oh, yeah, that guy has this obsession for getting people off the streets. And he does it through any means necessary. Oh, and he gets with the prosecutor and tries to push for the max sentence too."

"How much time did your client get?"

"I got the judge to give her ten years and five years' probation."

"That's a long time."

"It was a lot better than getting forty years. That was the max the judge could've given her. Ten was the minimum for the amount of drugs she was in possession of."

"Damn! If he's like that behind a drug charge, I wonder how he is in pursuing a murder conviction."

"Trust me, you wouldn't want to know."

Rosenberg and I talked for a few more minutes. After he got my information, he escorted me up to the reception area and had me pay the receptionist the up-front cost of $1,500 to escort me to the precinct. After he bade me farewell, he greeted his client Greg and then they disappeared into his office. Once I had made my credit card payment, I was given a receipt and Mr. Rosenberg's card.

"How is your schedule these next few days?" the receptionist asked me.

"I'm free."

"Okay, well, give me a day to call you with the time and day to meet Mr. Rosenberg at the homicide division of the Chesapeake Police Department."

"I'll wait for your call," I assured her.

"Thank you. And have a nice day."

"You too," I said, and then I exited the building.

As soon as I got inside my car, I sat there and felt a sense of relief. It finally felt like I wasn't alone. Hiring the attorney to accompany me to speak with the cops lifted a load from my shoulders. Having him by me would definitely keep me out of jail. And knowing this would allow me to get a good night's rest.

I couldn't get in the house fast enough when my cell phone rang. I looked down at the caller ID and saw that my brother, Alonzo, was calling me. While I was letting myself inside the front door, I took his call. By the time I said hello, listened to the recording, and pressed the number 5 button, I had stepped out of my shoes, laid my purse down, and had crawled on my bed.

"What's up, little sis?" he greeted me.

"I'm doing better now," I said with an upbeat tone.

"Okay, that sounds positive. Tell me what happened." Alonzo got straight to the point.

"Well, I took your advice and went to see an attorney today."

"What's his name?"

"Rosenberg."

"Is he at the same firm as my attorney?"

"Yes."

"So, what did he say?"

"Well, I'm going to let him accompany me to the precinct to talk to the detectives first and see where it goes from there."

"So you hired him?"

"Well, yeah, to go there and be with me while I answer the detectives' questions."

"How much is he charging you?"

"Well, he's only charging me fifteen hundred to accompany me to the interview. And if by any chance the cops want to come back and charge me with a crime, then his hourly rate is four hundred."

"Damn! That's more than what my lawyer charges."

"I know. I said the same thing. But that's not it, my attorney's retainer is five grand more than what your attorney charges."

"What the fuck is wrong with this dude? Does he think people just walk around with that kind of money?"

"I think he does."

"I don't know, Alayna. That's a lot of money."

"Yeah, I may need to shop around."

"Good idea," he agreed, and then he said, "Well, I finally got that visit you mentioned that would probably happen."

"Oh, really?" I said, shocked.

"Yeah, and they both tried to grill me for information about you too."

"What did they say?"

"They wanted to know if you killed Tim. I said, of course not. Then they asked if you were capable of hiring someone to do it. I told them that was impossible as well. And then those motherfuckers had the audacity to ask me if I'd killed those people I was in jail for!"

"And what did you say?"

"I laughed at them and then I stood up and yelled for the CO to come and get me. Because at that point I had heard enough of their bullshit."

"Wow! So they think that I could have had something to do with Tim's death! How fucked up is that?" I spat, knowing that my brother's phone calls were being recorded. So I had to play the part.

"Don't take it personal. They're just fishing. When they don't have any leads, they tend to point fingers at anyone caught at the scene of the crime."

"Well, they need to point their fingers elsewhere."

"Don't sweat it. Once they realize that they are wasting their time on you, they'll move on and find the person who actually did it."

"They better, because I don't need the headache."

"I feel you," Alonzo said. Then he changed the subject. "So he's four hundred dollars an hour, huh?"

I realized he was talking about the attorney. "Yup."

"Charging that much, he's gotta be good."

"Your attorney recommended him."

"He's got to be a senior partner."

"I would assume so."

"Well, let's see how he handles things when y'all go down there and talk to those detectives."

"I'm with you on that," I agreed, because the proof was in the pudding. Seeing how he would protect me against those monsters at the precinct was going to say a lot. It might even dictate whether or not I used him to represent me if murder charges were filed against me. Hopefully, it didn't come to that. But I would see.

CHAPTER 18

Jesse

*I*T WAS MY TURN TO WASH DISHES AT THE STATION TODAY, SINCE PAUL cooked everyone spaghetti. After putting away the pots and pans and wiping down the tables and countertops in the kitchen, I retired to the TV lounge area to watch a little bit of television. The movie *World War Z* was playing, and Mike was front and center.

"Is it good?" I asked.

Mike was so engrossed in the film that when he answered me, he didn't take his eyes off the television. "Yeah."

"What is it about?"

"Zombies."

"Oh, wow!" I commented. I wasn't into the whole zombie thing, but that was all the rage on television. It seemed like every time you turned on the TV, you saw *The Walking Dead, Fear the Walking Dead, Tales of the Walking Dead*, you name it. Someone was dead.

Now as I began to watch this movie unfold, Special Agent McGee and Special Agent Fletcher walked in. They were both escorted into the lounge area by Paul. He pointed me out and McGee asked if she could speak to me privately. I obliged and walked into the hallway with them. Paul stayed in the TV lounge area with Mike.

Surprised by their visit, I stood there and waited for them to start the dialogue. "Is there somewhere we can sit and talk in a more private setting?"

"Well, I don't have an office, but you can come to my room," I volunteered.

"Okay, yeah let's do that," Agent McGee insisted.

I led the way to my room, and after we entered, Agent McGee took a seat on the chair next to my small desk, while the other agent stood up next to her. I sat down on my bed.

"So I know you're wondering why we're here?" she started off.

I nodded my head and said yes.

"Well, we're here for a few reasons. You already know we're investigating the insurance fraud and murder case of Alonzo Riddick, and Tim was helping us with that, but, unfortunately, he's no longer with us . . ."

I sighed heavily. "Yeah."

"Speaking of which . . . the homicide detectives investigating that case spoke with you, right?"

"Yes, we spoke extensively," I assured her, giving the agents an ogling expression. "Have you spoken with them?" I threw the question back at them. I wanted to see if we were on the same page.

"Yes, we've spoken with them on several occasions. Why do you ask?" She became inquisitive.

"I told them that I believed Alayna had something to do with Tim's murder. She's behind it."

Agent McGee smiled at me and then looked at her partner. They both smiled at one another and then she looked back at me.

"Do tell," she coached me.

"Look, the night he left out of here, I told him not to go. But being the stubborn person he is, he did it anyway. Talking about how she really needed to talk to him about something important. And then fast-forward a few hours later, he's dead. Now tell me that wasn't a setup?" I pointed out.

"So you think she had Tim killed?"

"Yes, I do."

"Why do you think that?"

"I can give you two reasons."

"I'm listening."

"Number one, I believe that she figured that if she couldn't have him, then no one else could. And second, I believe that she wanted Tim out of the way so he wouldn't testify against Alonzo."

McGee and her partner looked at one another again. "Is this your theory?"

"This is what I know."

"And you have proof of this?" she wanted to know.

"No, but I've heard things. Tim and I talked a lot."

"Did Tim tell you that he feared for his life?"

"Let me say it this way . . ." I started off, and then I paused to gather my thoughts. "When he found out that Alonzo killed those people, he thought that he would be next."

"So you believe that Alonzo murdered those people?"

"Who else could've done it?"

"Alonzo said that Tim murdered those people."

"Ah . . . come on now! That's bullshit! And you believed him?" I gabbled. I was becoming irritated that she would utter those words out of her mouth.

She held up both of her hands. "Hey, don't shoot the messenger," she commented.

"I'm sorry if I'm getting a little teed off, but I'm just a bit frustrated that everyone is dragging their feet with this investigation."

"You mean the one we're working on?" Agent Fletcher chimed in.

"No, I'm talking Tim's murder."

"Well, we don't have jurisdiction over that one. But we're following it very closely because it involved our witness. Speaking of which, we're also here because one of our other witnesses in our case was just murdered last night."

"No fucking way!" I blurted out. I was immediately consumed with shock.

"You haven't heard?"

"No,"

"Well, it was the witness who said they saw Alonzo leaving the first murder victim's house the day he was killed. They were going to testify in Alonzo's trial. But that's not gonna happen now," Agent McGee explained.

I swear, I couldn't believe it. The one person who could ID Alonzo was now dead. What the hell was going on? "So, what happens now? Alonzo just walks away scot-free?"

"Oh, no. He's not going anywhere with anything."

"So, was this witness a man or a woman?"

"It was a woman. Her name was Lori White. She was the victim's neighbor."

"When was she murdered?"

"Last night."

"In her home?"

"She was on her way inside her home when she was killed."

"What happened?"

"We're still trying to figure that out right now. Once again, we stopped by because we were hoping that you heard something about it. Maybe there was a connection between this woman and Tim," Agent McGee said as she searched my face.

But I didn't know what to tell her. I didn't have anything. I had no idea that their witness was dead. It seemed like everyone connected to Alonzo was dying and they needed to do something about it.

"I betcha Alayna knows who murdered that lady," I voiced my opinion.

"Think so?" Agent Fletcher spoke up.

"Absolutely! I mean, why else would that poor woman get killed? It wasn't because she was at the wrong place at the wrong time."

"Does anyone here talk to Alonzo?" Agent McGee wanted to know.

"Not to my knowledge."

"Has Alayna visited this place recently?"

"Nope. She hasn't been here."

Agent McGee let out a long sigh. She looked defeated. "Well, I'll tell you what, if you hear anything, you give us a call," she insisted, and then she handed me a card she pulled from the inside of her jacket pocket. "That means *anything*."

I took the business card and folded it into my hand. "Will do," I assured them.

As both agents were leaving my room, Agent McGee asked if they could go back into Tim's office and look around again. I said sure and escorted them there. After I let them in, I warned them that Tim's wife had been by and had taken a few things out of there. They thanked me and I left them alone.

CHAPTER 19

Kirsten

I CAUGHT MYSELF TRYING TO GET A NAP, BUT MY HOME PHONE started to ring. I looked at my cell phone and saw that it was a little after 4:00 p.m. I yelled for one of my kids to answer it, but they ignored me; that left me no choice but to answer it. If I didn't, it wasn't going to stop ringing.

"Hello," I finally said after snatching the receiver up from the base of the phone port. I instantly heard a pre-recorded message coming through the phone telling me there was an inmate calling from Virginia Beach Regional Jail. It gave me the inmate's name and then they forewarned me the call would be monitored. Finally they told me that if I agreed to the terms, to press the number 5 button. I did and then waited for the person on the other side to speak first, because, for one, I was shocked to get this call, and two, I wondered what he had to say after all this time.

"Hello, is this Kirsten?" he asked.

I hesitated for a moment, trying to figure out how to approach this. I didn't want to come off like a bitch, because I wanted to hear what he had to say. But then something inside of me was nagging me about his possible involvement in my husband's murder. So, how could I be objective, but at the same time let him know that I wouldn't tolerate any of his bullshit while we were on this phone call? I would have to play it by ear.

"Yes, this is Kirsten," I finally replied.

"Hey, how you doing? This is Alonzo," he said. I could tell he was nervous.

"I know who it is. How can I help you?" I got straight to the point.

"Well, I know it's been a long time since we last seen one another. And I know there's been a lot of talk going around about some things that I'm supposed to have done, but I didn't call you about that. I called because I heard about what happened to Tim and I wanted to offer my condolences to you and your family."

"You know he loved you like a brother, right?" I stated and waited for his answer.

"Yes, I did. And I loved him too, Kirsten. He took me underneath his wing after my father died."

"Yes, Alonzo, he did."

"So . . . so, how are you and the kids holding up?" he wanted to know.

"Well, they're not doing so good. But we'll get through it together."

"Look, I know that the FBI wanted Tim to testify against me, so I want to be the first to tell you that I don't have any ill will against him because of that. And that my love for him hasn't changed one bit."

"That's nice," I replied sarcastically. "But tell me, where were you when your sister was having an affair with my husband?" I asked through gritting teeth.

"Kirsten, I swear, I don't know where I was. Because, best believe me, if I would've known, I would've stopped it right then and there."

"Well, tell me why she met him the night he was murdered?

113

Tell me why she felt it was so important to have him go to that dark junkyard that time of the night, where those men were able to rob and kill him in cold blood?" My questions continued as I grinded my teeth together.

"Kirsten, I wish that I could answer that question."

"What do you mean, you 'wish' you 'could answer that question'? What's stopping you?"

"I don't have the answer."

"So you mean to tell me that you haven't spoken to your sister since my husband has been dead?"

"Yes, I've spoken to her a few times. But I can't get a word out of her. She's really traumatized about all this," he tried to reason.

"That's crap and you know it, Alonzo. That hussy set my husband up and had him killed."

"No, no, no, Kirsten! Alayna wouldn't do anything like that. She's just not that type of person."

"That's not what Jesse said. He said that he knows for a fact she had my husband killed. And I believe him."

"Kirsten, Jesse doesn't know what he's talking about. He's a misguided individual."

"He can't be that misguided. Believe me, he knows a lot more than you think."

"Kirsten, he's poisoning your mind."

"Well, at least he had the decency to give me the rundown on your sleazy-ass sister," I snapped. This guy was plucking my nerves with his nonchalant behavior. It was getting underneath my skin.

"Kirsten, I'm not going to sit on this phone and let you bash my sister," he stated calmly, and then he ended the call.

"Hello," I said, and all I got in return was dead air. I immediately placed the phone receiver back in the base holder.

"Fucking asshole!" I shouted.

CHAPTER 20

Pricilla

S EVERAL DAYS LATER, MY MAMA INVITED ME OVER TO DINNER TO patch things up from the accusations she made about Alonzo's murder case while she was at my house. I declined the offer at first, but when she said she was making my favorite five-cheese lasagna, I had to reconsider. She welcomed me with open arms when I walked into her home. She had the red carpet rolled out for me. She had music playing. The food was smelling good. And to top things off, she handed me a glass of red wine as soon as I entered the kitchen. I smiled and took the glass in my hand.

"Thank you, Mommy!" I said, and then I took a sip. The fruitiness of the wine engulfed my taste buds. It was chilled and so delicious. "Is this cabernet?" I wondered aloud.

My mother smiled after she took a sip from her glass. "Why, of course, it is," she acknowledged.

I sat down on one of the barstools placed in front of the island in her kitchen. While she was climbing on the barstool next to me, the front door opened and in came my brother, K-Rock, and his friend Russell. They both looked like they had done an all-nighter in the trap house. As they approached us, I noticed them both taking in the aroma of my mother's food.

"I see y'all sniffing the air like dogs," I commented, and chuckled.

"You leave my baby alone, Pricilla," my mother teased as she stood a few feet away from me with arms extended to embrace my brother.

K-Rock smiled. "Yeah, you heard what Mama said. Leave me alone," he commented, relishing the moment. He embraced my mother with a warm hug and a kiss on the cheek.

"I'ma leave you alone, all right," I fired back jokingly. "What's up, Russell?"

"Nothing much, Cilla, what's up with you?" he asked as he waited next to K-Rock. When K-Rock released my mother, Russell hugged her next.

"How are you doing, baby?" she spoke to Russell as they embraced.

"I'm doing good, Mrs. Gates. Smells like me and K came at the right time," he noted after hugging her.

"Yeah, Mama, whatcha cooking?" K wanted to know as he looked over at the stove.

"Oh, a little lasagna that I whipped up for me and your sister."

"Yep, it is *just* for me and her," I made known.

"Oh, stop blocking," K whined in a playful manner.

"What brings you guys by?" Mama got straight to the point.

"I stopped by to see how you were doing," he replied.

"Well, I'm doing great," she said as she made her way back over to the barstool. "I asked your sister to come over so we can have some girl time," she added as she slid up on the stool.

"I guess that's our cue, Russell."

"You guys can take some food to go," my mother offered.

"Oh, cool! Yeah, let's do that," Russell said eagerly.

"I'll take it," K agreed as he made his way over to the area of the kitchen where my mother kept her plastic containers. He grabbed a Tupperware bowl from the cabinet and walked over to the stove, with the posture that he was going to pack some of the food away into his container. Russell stood near me and watched from afar.

"You better wash your hands first," my mother barked.

"Mom, why don't you serve him yourself?" I suggested.

See, my brother was a street hustler. His day consisted of selling drugs, handling money, touching different stolen items, and shaking different people's hands. So, in other words, his hands were not clean, and it would behoove my mother to take the reins in this matter so he wouldn't be spreading germs and a whole bunch of bacteria around.

My mom took my advice and helped my brother with his food. She even packed some away for Russell. While the food-filled containers were being exchanged from hand to hand, K inquired about Alonzo.

"Zo got a court date yet?" he started off.

"Well, he's already been to his preliminary hearing. So we're trying to figure out if we're going to do a jury trial or allow the judge to decide his fate," I explained.

"I think you should let a judge decide," Russell interjected.

"Nah, a jury would be better," K disagreed. "What do you think, Mama?" K asked my mother.

"I'm staying out of that one," she replied.

I immediately shot her a harsh look. I mean, I only came over here because she wanted to make amends with me for how she talked about Alonzo. But from the comment she just made, it seemed as though she really did feel like Alonzo killed those people. I wondered how she'd answer that question if I wasn't here.

"Mom, what do you mean by that?" I asked aloud. I couldn't hold it back.

"Nothing, darling."

"So, why are you staying out of it?" I pressed.

"Because I really don't have an opinion on it," she responded calmly. I could tell that she didn't want to open up another can of worms.

"What's wrong with you today?" My brother directed this question at me.

"Nothing. I'm just trying to figure out where Mom is on all of this," I said.

"Well, like I said before, I don't have an opinion on it. I choose to be neutral and that's where I'm going to stay," she replied adamantly.

My brother saw chaos brewing, so he immediately intervened. "Come on and let me holla at you," he said, grabbing my hand and helping me off the barstool. He led me outside on the front porch of my mother's house. As soon as he closed the front door behind us, he opened dialogue.

"What's going on?"

I took a deep breath and exhaled. "I'm sure you already know this, but Mama thinks that Alonzo killed those people."

"Shit, me too!"

"Come on now, K, that's fucked up!"

"You want me to keep it one hundred, don't you?"

"Yeah, but damn!"

"I mean, come on, sis, look at it like this. Those mu'fuckas owed him some bread, and when they didn't want to pay up, he did what he had to do." My brother spoke nonchalantly, but more like mindlessly in my head—and I didn't like it. It really rubbed me the wrong way.

"That's messed up that y'all are thinking that way. I mean, it's bad enough that the Feds are against him and trying everything in their power to lock him up for the rest of his life, but to hear that my own family also believes he's guilty is heartbreaking. He has no one else in his corner left, but me and his sister."

"Whether you believe it or not, I'm in his corner. And you will find that out soon enough," he mentioned.

"What do you mean?"

"I ain't got nothing else to say. Just know that I'm working behind the scenes and I'm rooting for him," he explained.

Unsure as to what he meant, I probed him. "What do you mean, you're 'working behind the scenes'?" I needed clarification.

"Just know that I know people. I know people who can get shit done out here, and I know people who can get shit done where he's at, so he's going to be good either way. Stop worrying. He's going to be fine. Now forget about how Mom feels about this whole situation and move on."

"Easy for you to say," I said after looking at K-Rock strangely. I wanted to ask more questions, but I opted not to do that. I figured he'd either lie or not tell me anyway, so what was the use?

"Trust me, it's simple. Now let's got back in the house," he insisted as he grabbed my hand and led me back into the house.

CHAPTER 21

Alonzo

"*P*OLICE SAY THEY FOUND DEANA SHEPARD LYING FACE *down on her front lawn late last night after her husband discovered her body after hearing two gunshots from his bedroom window. Deana Shepard was a thirty-three-year-old bank teller, wife, and mother of two. The husband broke his silence today with the assistance of her family's attorney," the reporter stated.*

"My wife was a beautiful woman and loving mother. She didn't ask for this. We lived quiet lives, and we didn't bother nobody. Now this message is for who killed my wife. I know this had something to do with our neighbor's murder. She didn't deserve to be killed like this . . . shot in the head like a vicious dog. The person who took her life will pay with the full extent of the law! I can guarantee you that!" Shepard's husband shouted at the reporter.

"There you have it, folks. The husband of the slain victim has spoken, and he and the investigating detectives are asking for your help. So, if you have any information, please call 1-800-LOCK-U-UP! Your call will remain anonymous. And there's a one-thousand-dollar cash reward if your infor-

*mation leads to an arrest. We will continue to follow the
story as it develops. I'm Sue Park, News Four."*

"Damn! Motherfuckers are dropping like flies around here,"
I commented loud enough for only myself to hear as I sat on the
metal bench in the cell block.

But I guess I didn't say it low enough, because my cellie,
Wayne, heard me.

"Ain't that where they said you killed that old man?" he asked.

I looked over my shoulders with a casual facial expression. My
first thought was to tell him to mind his fucking business. But
then I realized that I was talking to a young car thief who had no
scruples whatsoever. There are no moral codes with this guy, so
I can't expect him to keep his mouth closed about my business
in a cell block full of noisy motherfuckers listening to every
word being uttered from anyone that'll open their mouths.

Okay, it was just him and me in the TV area, but niggas were
within feet of us lying in their beds with their blankets covering
their faces, but that didn't mean they were asleep. Trust me,
those niggas were eavesdropping like a motherfucker. So I
played it cool and acted like I didn't know what this little nigga
was talking about.

"Nah, I don't think so," I finally said, and then I got up and
walked to my cell.

I thought he was going to follow me, but he got on the nearest phone and made a call out. I climbed on my bunk and went
into a zone and thought about what was going to happen from
here. What I really wanted to do was get on the phone and call
my sister, but I knew that wouldn't be a good idea. I needed to
be cool and let this thing play out. I mean, at this point, why
touch it? It was obvious that Alayna took care of that loose end,
and it was beginning to look like I was home free.

* * *

"Riddick, get ready! You've got an attorney visit," the CO yelled from the hallway of the cell block.

It seemed like I was always lying on my bed when the CO shouted my name; so like clockwork, I got up from my bunk, slipped on my shoes, and headed out of my cell. I didn't have to wonder why my attorney was here to see me today. I had just seen the news coverage on television and that witness had a direct connection to my case, so maybe my lawyer was here to tell me that I was on my way out of here. Hearing that would be like music to my ears.

"Open cell block 8-B," the CO radioed the command pod. Seconds later, the door slid open, so I stepped in the small cage and watched as the first door closed. Immediately the second cell door on the opposite side of me opened, which allowed me to step into the hallway. "Turn toward the wall," the CO instructed me.

So I turned and faced the wall and that's when he handcuffed my wrists behind my back. After that, he led me out of the cell block and into a nearby corridor. For some odd reason I was feeling good about this visit. Good news was definitely around the corner.

The walk to the attorney and inmate visiting room was a hop, skip, and a jump away. We got there in no time. When the CO opened the door and escorted me inside, I was taken aback at what I saw. There, standing on the other side of the small metal table, were both of my archnemeses.

"Well, well, well, if it isn't Mr. Alonzo Riddick," Special Agent McGee announced as the CO pushed me farther into the room.

"Nah, I ain't trying to talk to y'all," I replied as I tried to stop the CO from pushing me toward the agents. I planted my feet into the cement floor, but my weight was no match for the CO's—not when I was wearing jailhouse slippers.

"Hey, hey, stop that," the CO instructed me as he pushed his body weight into my back.

"What are you doing, Alonzo? What, ya don't want to see us?" She laughed. It was a hearty, maniacal laugh.

"What the fuck is so funny?" I asked her. "And you don't have to take off my cuffs, because I'm not staying in here and talking to these assholes," I told the CO.

"I just stopped by to congratulate you on getting rid of two of my most important witnesses," she said.

"I don't know what you're talking about," I said, shrugging my shoulders. At this point talking to these agents was off-limits, especially while my attorney wasn't around. And when I thought about it, it didn't matter if my attorney was present. I *still* didn't have shit to say to these motherfuckers.

"Oh, you know fully well what I'm talking about. First it was Tim and now Deana Shepard. An innocent mother of two, on her way into her home with a couple bags of groceries in her hands, and then *boom*! Two shots to the head because she witnessed your sorry ass coming out of Mr. Cole's house after you murdered him . . ."

"I didn't murder him. And I didn't have shit to do with Tim's murder, or that lady you just mentioned. This is all a misunderstanding. Or maybe she was cheating on her husband with another man and the dude killed her," I responded nonchalantly. I knew I couldn't get mad at these idiots. This stunt they were pulling was out of desperation. They were losing their case, so they got to do whatever was necessary to keep it alive.

Agent McGee came rushing around the table, grabbed my collar, and pulled me face-to-face with hers. She exhaled a windstorm of breath. She knew that I was full of shit.

"You fucking piece of shit! I know you and your sister had Tim and Deana Shepard murdered, so you can deny it until your face turns blue. And I'm going to prove it, if it takes the last breath out of me," she gritted.

Then, out of nowhere, the door flung open and my attorney, Jeff Swartz, swooped in. "That's enough, Agent McGee, let my client go at this moment," my attorney instructed this unstable-ass woman. "Unhand him, or do you want me to make a phone call?"

She hesitated until my attorney reminded her of the laws that restricted her from touching a defendant who's currently on trial. Slowly she loosened her grip on me.

"You better put some sense into this murderer's head before I do," she threatened after she let me go, and stepped backward.

"I thought you were supposed to wait for me at the front of the jail before coming back here with my client? That was what we agreed upon," Swartz stated.

"We were told that you were back here, so that's why we came," she replied. But I could tell that she was lying through her fucking teeth. That bitch knew that my attorney wasn't here.

"That's bullshit! She knew what she was doing. She wanted to beat you back here so she could get me alone before you got here!" I roared.

"You don't know shit!" she challenged me.

"I know enough, believe me," I told her, and gritted my teeth at her—all while still in handcuffs and the CO standing along-side of me.

"Look, this interview is over," my attorney announced. "You and your partner may leave so that I can speak to my client in private."

"This ain't over," Agent McGee said.

"Oh, yes, it is, Agent. Now leave at once," my attorney snapped.

Agent Fletcher grabbed Agent McGee by the arm and pulled her back in his direction. "Come on, let's go," he said.

Agent McGee followed her partner's lead and allowed him to escort her out of the room. On her way past the metal table, she shot one last look at me and then she overturned the chair. *CLANG! CLING! CLANG!*

The chair bounced around on the floor until it stopped. My

attorney picked up the chair and placed it back at the table. "Uncuff him, please," my attorney demanded of the CO.

After I was completely uncuffed, I sat down in the chair and started readjusting the collar of my jail-issued jumpsuit.

"You can leave us now," my attorney added, instructing the CO to leave me in there with him, after seeing both agents had left before him.

Immediately after the door was closed and locked, Swartz placed his briefcase down on the opposite side of the metal table and he got down to business.

"I can only assume that they told you why they were here to see you?" he started off.

"Yeah, they accused me of having the lady who got shot last night killed. They think I had something to do with Tim's murder too."

"Yeah, I know. So, what did you say to them?"

"I said nothing. I told her that I didn't know what she was talking about."

"Good. Keep it that way."

"So, what does that mean for my case?"

"Well, it means that I'm in a position to file a motion to suppress certain evidence in your case."

"How does that work?"

"A motion to suppress evidence is generally requested by a defendant's attorney asking the judge to exclude certain evidence from trial. Right now is the time to do it, and if we win it, the prosecution or judge may have to dismiss the case."

"No fucking way!" I said with excitement.

"Hold up! Let's not get too excited. It may not happen that way. But it is possible."

"What's the worst-case scenario?"

"Well, the judge could only throw out some things and then we would still have to move forward to the trial phase."

"What other witnesses do they have?"

"That's the thing, right now they don't. Tim and Deana Shepard were their only witnesses, and that would be our argument for the motion to suppress."

"What about the fraud charges?"

"The U.S. attorney planned on using Tim's testimony on those charges, and as of right now, no one has come forward to say they entered into an agreement with you guys to defraud their insurance company."

"Yes!" I belted out a breath of fresh air and excitement.

"But again . . . let's not get excited. I have seen cases where the prosecutor will bring out a witness at the last minute and blow the case wide open. So let's play it safe until we are out of the woods."

"Sounds good."

Back in the cell block, word had already gotten back that I had gotten roughed up by the federal agents. My cellie, Wayne, met me at the entryway of the cell with a lot to say. "You a'ight?" he started off.

"Yeah, why?" I asked after sliding by him to get inside.

"The CO came back here and told everybody that a female agent jacked you up a little bit. He said that he had to tell her to step back," he continued.

"He's a fucking liar. When that bitch grabbed me by my collar, that cracker didn't do shit, and that motherfucker kept the cuffs on me too," I explained as I sat down on my bed.

Wayne chuckled. "Man, I can't believe that dude lied like that. Yo, he had niggas in there thinking that homegirl jacked you up for talking shit to her and he had to stop her."

"Yeah, he straight lied about that one."

"So, what happened?"

"Well, I thought I was going in the room to see my lawyer, but when I get in there, I see the federal agents who are prosecuting my case. So, off the bat, you know I'm not trying to see them, so I tell the CO to bring me back to the block. But homegirl gets in my face and accuses me of a bunch of shit. I tell her I ain't did nothing, and that she's gonna have to prove it, so she goes off and charges me. She grabs me by the collar and gets in my face. Now I'm laughing at her because she's really in her feelings and she get angry. She starts talking shit, and the CO just stood there and said nothing. Thank God my lawyer comes through the door and stops her. Because she was off her rocker."

"You know females are really sensitive, especially if they can't get their way."

"Yeah, tell me about it," I agreed, instantly thinking about Pricilla. I needed to call her and tell her the news that my attorney gave me, so I abruptly got up from the bed.

"Where you going?" my cellie wanted to know.

"I've got to make a phone call," I told him, and made my way past him.

Thankfully, there was a phone available, because I was not in the mood to wait around to use the phone. After I dialed Pricilla's number, I waited for her to answer.

"Hello," she said.

"Hey, pretty lady!"

"Sounds like you're in a good mood," she pointed out.

"Kinda, sort of."

"What's up?"

"Well, first off, I had a run-in with the Feds not too long ago."

"What do you mean?"

"They came down here to the jail to talk to me, but they came back here without my lawyer being present. So, when I walked into the room with the CO, the female agent tried to trick me up and get me to say that I have something to do with Tim's murder. Yo, she was bugging out! She even got in my face and acted like she wanted to hit me. I started laughing and she got really mad."

"What did the guard do when all of this was going on?"

"That cracker didn't do shit. He just let her do her thing. It was crazy."

"So nobody did anything?"

"Nope, but luckily, my lawyer came in there not too long after. And as soon as he saw her in my face, he told her to step back before he made a phone call that she ain't gonna like."

"And did she listen?"

"Hell yeah, she listened and then he told her to get out the room."

"Did she go?"

"She didn't have a choice," I said cheerfully. "And you should've seen her face when her partner was pulling her out of the room. Man, it was priceless."

"I can't believe that she carried on the way she did."

"Baby, she was flipping out, talking about she knows I was behind it, and that just because Tim's dead, doesn't mean I am not going to go down for a long time. I mean, she was at my throat."

"And she said all of this before your lawyer walked in?"

"Yup."

"So, did you tell him what she said?"

"Yeah, I told him, and he said that he's going to file a motion tomorrow, and that motion might bring me home sooner than we think," I began to explain.

I didn't want to tell her too much or tell her what motion he was going to file, because I knew that the phones were tapped, and I didn't want word to get back to the Feds. I figured all she needed to know was that I talked to my lawyer and things were looking good for me.

"That sounds promising."

"Yeah, I know."

"Did he say when this would happen?"

"I will know in a few days."

"That's awesome, baby. Sounds like we can get the show back on the road with the wedding plans," she suggested.

But I wasn't trying to get into all of that. Whether she knew it or not, the wedding was off the table for now. My days of wanting to get married were long gone.

"Let's not get ahead of ourselves. Let's just do one thing at a time, please," I insisted.

She sucked her teeth. "Yeah, whatever," she replied.

"So, where is everyone?"

"You mean *my mother?*"

"Not really, but I guess."

"She's home."

"You talked to my sister?"

"Not for a few days. I've been trying to call her, but her phone keeps going to voicemail."

"Go over to her house and check up on her. Tell her what I told you too," I urged.

"You mean about you coming home sooner?"

"Yeah. Listen, I want you to do me a favor."

"What is that?"

"When it's time for me to go to court, don't bring your mama."

"I don't think she wanted to come in the first place."

"Good, so then it's settled."

CHAPTER 22

Alayna

I FINALLY GOT THE CALL FROM MR. ROSENBERG'S RECEPTIONIST. DEtective Showers placed a manila folder down on the opposite side of the small, wobbly metal table directly in front of me. Detective Showers's face was stoic and hard-lined. He wore twenty-two years of police work like a mask, each worry line that cropped up near his mouth and wrinkle branching out from the corner of his eyes telling a different story of sleepless nights, dead people, and remorseless suspects.

They said that he had broken through the city of Chesapeake's glass ceiling and he prided himself on his nearly perfect track record. He was known around the department for "always getting his man." No kids, no family, and no life outside of work made it easy for him to be the best of the best. They also said he dedicated his entire adult life to the police department, sometimes to a fault. Since becoming a detective, he had not left any case unsolved and had elicited confessions in all but one of his cases.

"You ready to talk?" Detective Showers asked, folding his arms into one another, across his chest. Intimidation was a scare tactic that he had been best at performing.

130

"My client is only here to answer relevant questions," my lawyer, Rosenberg, interjected.

Detective Showers chuckled. "Are we here to talk about my murder investigation?" Showers wanted clarification.

"She's here to answer relevant questions. And I will choose which questions she will answer."

"Don't worry, all of my questions will be relevant," the detective replied, shifting his head to the side. He then unfolded his arms and flipped open the folder. Detective Showers peered down at the words, as if reading them, and then he closed the folder shut. I've heard that this was a scare tactic of his, having a suspect think he had more information on them than he really had.

As I sat there and watched Detective Showers put on a show in front of my attorney and me, I tried to play it cool. I was always told to stay calm and never let a person see you sweat—especially a cop.

"Alayna, on the night Tim Stancil was murdered, did you order that hit?"

Caught off guard with the detective's first question, I instantly clenched my fists together as the heat started rising from my feet, making its way up my body. I looked to Rosenberg for direction, and he gave me the head nod to answer the question. While my heart pounded rapidly inside my chest, I could feel adrenaline rushing through my veins. I wanted to punch a wall or kick something; the urges were overwhelming me. Thoughts were running through my mind and, of course, what I was thinking wasn't exactly the truth, but I couldn't get my mouth to open. I even contemplated doing sign language, but I couldn't move my arms. I was completely frozen. It was like I was having an out-of-body experience.

"Answer my question, Alayna. Did you kill Tim?"

That time Detective Showers's words stung like a wasp. I sat up in the chair and, without hesitation, denied having anything to do with Tim's murder.

"Of course not," I finally said.

"Then who did? Who shot and killed him?"

"I don't know. I couldn't see their faces. It was too dark," I explained.

"Well, take me back to the night of the murder. Walk us through that night. Detail every step you took from the time you two decided to meet at the salvage yard until the moment he was shot and killed."

"But we've already been over this before," I pointed out.

"I know. And I want to hear it again."

"But it's the same story," I protested, sitting up straight in the hard wooden chair, looking at the detective head-on.

"So let's hear it." He wouldn't let up. And then he turned his attention toward my attorney. "Will you please get your client to cooperate? Time is ticking," Detective Showers asked.

Rosenberg leaned in toward me and whispered in my ear, "Are you okay with repeating the story?"

I turned around and looked at him and then hunched my shoulders.

"Well, then, go ahead," he ushered me along.

I thought for a moment about where to start and then I took a deep breath and exhaled. "I called Tim that night and asked him if we could talk about our relationship. He told me that he didn't want to talk about it over the phone and that he'd rather meet in person," I started off. "So I said okay and asked him where he wanted to meet. He said for us to meet at that salvage yard. He was already there when I pulled up, so when I got out of my Jeep, he got out of his truck, and we met at the halfway point between our cars. He started the exchange with a compliment about how good I looked. I thanked him and then we started talking about us . . ."

"Let's hear it," Detective Showers probed.

"Well, as you already know, Tim and I were seeing one another—"

"Having an affair?"

"Yes, and we had called it quits earlier that day. Meeting that night was for the purpose of discussing where we were going from there. He said that he wanted to continue seeing me and I told him it was over. I was done. He said that he wasn't trying to hear that. We started going back and forth, and then out of nowhere two guys pop out from behind our cars, waving their guns at us and demanding money—"

"From you?"

"No, from Tim. Both guys surrounded him and demanded that he give them everything he had. Tim refused, they jumped him, and then they robbed him anyway."

"What were you doing that whole time?"

"I was screaming and yelling for Tim to give them whatever they were asking for, but he wouldn't listen to me. When they were done with him, they shot him and ran off," I relayed, looking directly at the detective to see if my story was making a dent in the doubt clouding the detective's face.

Detective Showers tilted his head and glared at me. He put his elbows on the table and leaned in. "Something about your story stinks to holy hell," he said and then he paused. "See, what I think is that you know a lot more than what you're letting on. I also believe you're a fucking liar from the bottom of your feet to the top of your head. One thing I know for sure is the truth will come out," he said seriously. It was like he wanted me to know that he wasn't a rookie. This wasn't his first time around the block on a homicide. But he stayed calm, though.

"I'm telling you the truth now," I said, annoyed. This guy was plucking my fucking nerves with this shit. I was ready to go and stood up on my feet.

"Where do you think you're going?" Showers retorted.

Rosenberg stood up beside me. "Is everything all right?" he whispered.

"I'm out of here," I told him.

The line had been drawn in the sand. The tension in the room was so thick, it was almost palpable.

"Oh, don't run now. Scared that you're going to slip up and tell us that you really murdered Tim?"

"That's enough, Detective. I think you are one step from being out of line. I know plenty of folks downtown at IAB, so you had better quit while you are ahead and leave us alone," Rosenberg said as he leaned across the table from the detective.

Detective Showers took heed and backed down. He held up his left hand, signaling his retreat, but his face said something totally different. It wasn't over. That was for sure. I had been forewarned that this detective was not going to quit until he had this case all ready for the prosecutors—and an indictment for the murder with my name on it.

Detective Showers chuckled. "You and I both know that she's guilty. Look at her, guilt is written all over her face," Detective Showers commented.

"Fuck you! You don't know shit!" I snapped, and then I turned and stormed out of the room.

I heard Rosenberg hurling threats at Detective Showers as the door to the room was closing. I contemplated finding the stairwell and taking the stairs, but I knew it would take me forever to get out of this building. So I rushed to the elevators and tapped the button. While I waited for the elevator door to open, large feelings of compunction started forming in the pit of my stomach. It was the worst case of anxiety ever. All I could think about was how the detectives were going to try everything in their power to lock me up. The thought of it was scary; so scary that the longer I stood here, the uneasier I felt.

I tapped the button again, as if that would make the elevator

134

come any faster, and I looked up at the light above the elevator doors and the down arrow on the left elevator door lit up white. Finally the doors dinged open and I immediately stepped inside. At that very moment a short-lived feeling of relief washed over me. I wasn't quite out of the building yet, but it felt like it. And with that feeling, as soon as the elevator door opened, I stepped off it and scurried out of the building.

I wanted to wait for Rosenberg, but I couldn't. I had to get away from this place as quickly as possible. I figured Rosenberg would call me before today was over, and I'd be waiting for his call.

Fifteen minutes into my drive home, I got a call from Rosenberg. His voice sounded alarming at first, but things settled down after he started explaining what was said after I left the precinct.

"Well, I will say that it didn't look good for you, walking out of there like that."

"What was I supposed to do? Just sit there and let him accuse me of something I didn't do?"

"That's what you paid me for. To be there and make sure that things were handled appropriately. Within legal ramifications."

"I felt harassed."

"I'm sure you did. Showers was asking you some harsh questions. But that's his job, Alayna."

"So, what happens now?" I wanted Rosenberg to get to the point.

"Well, it's obvious that the detectives don't have any suspects. Right now, they're fishing. See, you're their only hope for any answers, but you're not giving them what they want, so they're going to try to put pressure on you."

"What do you mean 'pressure'?"

"They're going to either come after you or someone close to you, since you're their only link to solving their case."

"But I've told them everything I know."

"But they feel that you're holding something back. They believe that you're involved somehow. They can't get past the part in your story when you said that the gunmen only attacked and robbed Tim, and not you. They're wondering why the murder suspects would leave you untouched. Unharmed."

"I don't know. I guess, maybe because I started screaming?"

"Well, if that's true, they're not buying it."

"Well, it's the truth," I lied. Just knowing that those jokers were going to be on me like a bloodhound didn't sit well with me. I wanted to be able to sleep at night. "So, what do I do now?"

"There's really nothing you can do if you don't know anything. So just sit tight. And I told them that if they need to speak with you again, to call me and I will call and let you know. But if for any reason, they try to contact you on their own, don't talk to them. You call me first."

"Okay, I will."

"Do you have any questions for me?"

"No, not at this moment."

"Okay, well, if you do, call the office and have my receptionist make an appointment for you."

"Gotcha!" I said.

"You have a nice day."

"Same to you."

CHAPTER 23

Pricilla

J UST AS I WAS INSTRUCTED, I GOT IN MY CAR AND DROVE OVER TO Alayna's house to check on her. I was shocked to see Levi in the house when she opened the door.

"Hey, what's up? Did I catch you at a bad time?" I asked her as I stood at the front door.

I could see him gathering some things up from the floor of the hallway, near the kitchen. And the last time I spoke with her, she had indicated she had told Levi she wanted a divorce and that he had to leave the house. So to see him here right now was surprising.

"No, you're good. Come on in," she insisted, and moved to the side so I could walk by her.

After she closed the front door and locked it, I followed her down the hallway in the direction of where Levi was. The tension in the air was really thick. I could tell they had just had a heated argument, so I didn't know how to approach the situation. The only thing I could think to do was speak, and that's what I did.

"Hey, Levi, long time no see," I broke the silence.

"Yeah, I know, it has been a minute, huh?" he replied, forcing a smile on his face as he lifted a bag over his shoulders.

I exhaled. "Yup," I said, and then I looked at Alayna, who was acting like Levi wasn't in the room at all.

He took a deep breath and exhaled. "Well, I guess that's my cue," he said.

"Wait, you're leaving so soon?" I asked, even though he had made it obvious when he lifted his bag over his shoulder. For some reason I wanted him to feel like his presence would be missed, when that was far from the truth.

"Yeah, I gotta head back over to my mother's house. Just had to stop over here to pick up a few things. But it was nice seeing you," he stated, and then he moved on by me.

"Nice seeing you too," I told him, and watched him leave.

I also watched Alayna follow behind him, while I took a seat on the sofa. I thought they were going to exchange words before he walked out of the door, but they didn't. It was so quiet, you could hear a pin drop. After she closed the front door and locked it, she returned to the living-room area, where she immediately dove right into why Levi was there.

"Do you know he had the nerve to ask me to give our marriage another try?" she mentioned as she plopped down on the sofa next to me.

"What did you say?"

"I told him that ship has sailed."

"And what did he say?"

"He didn't say anything."

"So, you're really going to go through a divorce?"

"You damn right, skippy. His ass has got to go. And the quicker I do it, the quicker I can be a single woman." She smiled; she seemed very happy at the idea.

"Seems like you've got it all sorted out."

"I do."

"Well, your brother wanted me to come by and check on you. Make sure you were fine."

"When did you talk to him?"

"A couple hours ago."

"What else is he talking about?"

"Well, he said that he might be coming home sooner than he thinks. His lawyer came by to see him and told him that he's going to file a motion. And if the judge grants it, he could be coming home."

"What kind of motion?"

"He didn't say. But he seemed very excited about it. He did tell me not to get my hopes up. But it sounds like it might be the real thing."

"That's great," Alayna said with excitement.

"I know. I am happy as hell. Can't wait to get back into re-vamping our wedding plans."

"Have you thought about a new date?"

"Not yet. Every time I bring it up, Alonzo shoots it down. It's like he wants to take care of the situation first and then we discuss getting married after he comes home."

"Well, that's understandable."

"Yeah, but no girl wants to hear her man tell her he doesn't want to talk about their wedding day. Its kind of, like, puts a bad taste in my mouth, if that makes sense."

"Yeah, I understand. But you've got to put yourself in his shoes. Having this case hanging over his head, with his life in the hands of a judge and jury, he doesn't have the headspace to think about his wedding day. You know men, they can only do one thing at a time."

I took a deep breath and exhaled. "Mmm, I guess you're right. But believe me, I didn't want to hear that at the time. You know I get really sensitive about my wedding."

Alayna chuckled. "You know I know!" she blurted out.

"Everybody knows." I laughed with her. "So, what's up with you? Has the cops been around here lately?" I changed the subject.

"Well, the detectives that were investigating Tim's murder came by looking for me again so we can talk about that night again, and when they realized I wasn't home, they left their business card on my front door. So instead of calling them back, I told Zo about it, and he advised me to hire an attorney, so I did. And I had him accompany me to the Chesapeake Police Department so that those assholes could ask me questions about Tim's murder."

"So, when did you do this?"

"You mean, hire the attorney or talk to the cops?"

"Both."

"I hired the attorney a couple days ago and we went down to the precinct earlier today. I just got back home, as a matter of fact."

"So, how did it go?"

"It went horribly wrong. One of them just flat out accused me of either killing Tim or having someone else do it."

"No way!"

"Yes, girl, it was a shit show!"

"So, what did you say?"

"I told them the same thing that I did on the night of the shooting. But for some reason they don't believe me."

"What don't they believe?"

"They just keep questioning about why the robbers would only try to rob Tim, and not rob and murder me."

"That's a valid point," I agreed, and Alayna's face quickly turned sour.

"What do you mean?" She became defensive.

"I'm just saying that it's a valid point. I wondered the same thing. I mean, I'm glad that nothing happened to you. But at the same time, I thought about it," I tried to explain.

"Well, for your information, I can't tell you why they didn't attack me. I couldn't read their minds. All I know is when they got what they wanted from Tim, they shot him and ran off," she snapped. She was visibly upset.

"I'm sorry, Alayna. I didn't mean to upset you." I began to apologize and reached over to embrace her in a hug. She pushed my hands back.

"No, it's okay," she responded.

I could tell that she wasn't feeling me, or anything I had just said. It was obvious that I struck a chord with her.

"Do you still want to talk about it?" I asked her.

"Not really." She brushed me off and stood up on her feet. I watched her walk into her kitchen and grab a bottle of water from the refrigerator. "Want one?" she asked as she held a bottle up in the air.

"No thanks," I told her.

As she made her way back into the living room where I was, my cell phone rang. I looked down at the caller ID and noticed that it was my brother, K-Rock, so I answered it.

"Hello," I said.

"Hey, sis, where you at?"

"I'm over at Alayna's house."

"Whatcha doing over there?"

"Zo wanted me to come by and check on her, since I hadn't seen her in a while. Where you at?"

"I'm at your crib. Mama wanted me to come to your house and pick up her scarf she left over here. She said something about wanting to wear it when she goes to brunch with her friends in the morning."

"Well, you're going to have to wait until I get there, or I'll just go there, then get it and take it to her later on."

"Well, I'm not waiting around. So, yeah, come and get it and take it to her yourself," he insisted.

"All right, so where are you on your way to now?" I asked him.

"To my girl crib."

I chuckled at the notion that K-Rock said he had a girl. He had never claimed being in a relationship before.

"Wait, when did this happen?" I probed.

"Just recently."

"What is her name?"

"Carmen."

"Oh, that's pretty. How old is she?"

"She's my age."

"What does she do?"

"Now why you gotta know all that?"

"Because I'm your sister and I want to make sure that you're spending your time with someone of some substance."

I heard Alayna chuckle in the background. "Girl, please, he is a street dude," I heard her say.

I shot her a quick look, like *Don't talk about my brother.* She caught my look and changed her facial expression.

"Look, let me handle what's going on in my life and you handle what's going on in yours. Is Zo good?" He changed the subject.

"Yeah, he's good. He called me earlier and told me that the female federal agent who's on his case came up to the jail and cornered him in a room, talking about she knows that he had something to do with his coworker getting killed and that she's going to find out and make sure he pays for it."

"Wait, when did this happen?" I heard Alayna ask.

I attempted to turn around and answer her, but K-Rock chimed in and said, "Where was his lawyer when all of this was going on?"

I held my finger up, asking her to give me a minute. "His lawyer came a few minutes later. But by then, she had already had her way with him."

"That's fucked up! So, what did he say to her?"

"What else could he do? He just told her that he wasn't involved."

"Damn, that's messed up. Yo, when you speak to him again, you tell him to keep his head up."

"Okay, I will," I assured K-Rock.

As soon as I ended the call, Alayna was literally idling by, waiting for me to reiterate what transpired between Agent McGee and Alonzo.

"So tell me what happened?"

I honestly didn't feel like repeating myself. But I found myself doing it anyway. I took a deep breath and exhaled. "Well, the CO pulled Alonzo out of his cell, making him think that he was going to see his attorney, but when he went into the attorney visiting room, the Feds are there waiting on him. So he tells the CO to take them back to the block, but instead Agent McGee gets in his face and starts talking shit about him having something to do with Tim's murder. So, of course, Alonzo denied it, but that wasn't enough for the agent. She grabs him by his jumpsuit collar and roughs him up a little bit, all while she's in his face talking smack. The CO stands there and does absolutely nothing, but thank God his attorney rushes in the room and stops everything. The attorney threatens Agent McGee and makes her and her partner leave the room. And right after they left, his attorney told him that he's going to file a motion and see if the judge will let him out early."

"What kind of motion?"

"He didn't say. All he said is that if the judge granted it, he could come home a lot sooner."

"Damn, I wonder what kind of motion that is?" Alayna wondered aloud.

"I don't know. But I sure hope the judge grants it."

"I second that," Alayna agreed, and then she doubled back and brought up the part of my conversation where I talked about the federal agent grabbing Alonzo by the collar of his jumpsuit. "I can't believe that ho went up there to the jail and put her hands on my brother like that."

"Well, believe it, because it happened. But I sure wish that I was there. Because I would've punched her right in her face," I said, voicing my opinion.

"I probably would've punched the bitch in the face too. But she knew what she was doing by going up there and asking the CO to bring Zo in the room without his attorney."

"Yeah, she did," I continued, despising the fact that she did my fiancé wrong. Once again, I thanked God for his attorney, because he came in and saved the day.

I chilled over Alayna's house for another fifteen to twenty minutes until my mother called me to remind me that I needed to bring her scarf to her house, so I gave Alayna a hug, told her that I would check on her later, and then I said my goodbyes.

CHAPTER 24

Jesse

MIKE AND PAUL PUT ME ON OUTSIDE CLEANING DUTY TODAY, SO I was tasked with detailing the outside of the fire truck. While I was shining its metal grill, I heard a nice, subtle voice call out my name from behind. I looked up and there was Tim's wife, Kirsten, standing over my shoulder. I greeted her with a smile.

"How are you?" I said to her warmly.

She smiled back. "I'm doing fine. Just came up here to let you guys know that I'm having Tim's funeral services the day after tomorrow. Here's the address and time we're having his service, if you guys want to come," she said while handing me a business card from the cemetery where I figured Tim was being buried.

"Wait, is his service inside or out?" I asked.

"It's going to be a graveside service," she told me.

"Oh, okay. Well, I'm not sure about the other guys, but I will definitely be there," I vowed.

"Well, you just make sure you let them know."

"Oh, sure, I can do that," I assured her.

"Thank you," she said. Then she turned around to leave but hesitated to take the first step. I watched her closely and waited for her next move. And that's when she turned back around and faced me. She gave me the impression that she didn't know what to say, but then all of a sudden, she got up the gumption to open her mouth. Her first words were "Was my husband gay?"

Taken aback by her question, I stood there in shock. I clutched my imaginary pearls as my heart rate picked up speed and said "Oh, my" in my mind. She waited for me to answer her question, so I swallowed the spit I had lingering in my throat and finally said, "Where did you hear that?"

I wanted her to tell me where she got that information from, so I could figure out whether or not to tell her the truth. As badly as I wanted to tell her that he and I had an affair, and that Tim loved me, I didn't want to end up being the bad guy in Kirsten's eyes when Alayna was already doing a helluva job of it.

"Alayna told me. She told me that she was the least of my worries and I needed to be looking at you, because she and Alonzo caught you giving Tim a blow job in his office."

My heart thundered now, and brisk, cold air brushed over me. And then suddenly that same freezing-cold air hit my face like ice water. I closed my eyes to hold back the guilt.

"Are you okay?" she asked me.

I swallowed another round of spit in the back of my throat and then I opened my eyes back up and looked at Kirsten. "Yes, I'm fine," I lied.

I was a nervous wreck. I wasn't prepared to answer that question. But I knew that I had to, and there was no getting out of it.

"It's obvious to me that Alayna is trying to hurt you with those sick allegations. They caught me doing no such thing and I can't believe she said that to you. It's hurtful that she would resort to this kind of behavior. I mean, who goes around and tells someone's wife their husband was gay and they caught another man giving him a blow job? How insulting is that? And especially to me? I know one thing, I am going to pay that little hussy a visit and tell her off, once and for all," I finally managed to say.

Kirsten seemed so relieved with my response that she stood

straight up with a posture that she could take on the world. "No, no! You don't have to confront her about it. I knew she was lying when she was telling me."

"Are you sure? Because I will go over there before nightfall," I assured her. But in all honesty I wasn't going to waste my energy going back over to Alayna's house. I'd said everything that I needed to say to her, and more. Now I was going to let the authorities handle her.

"Yes, I'm sure. She's a miserable soul. Let her stay where she is, and I will stay where I am. She will get hers. And so will her brother. Speaking of which, he had the nerve to call me the other day."

"Wait, he called you?"

"Yep."

"And said exactly what?"

"He said he was sorry about Tim's death and wanted to give his condolences."

"So he said that he was sorry?"

"Yes."

"So, was that like an admission?" I asked, holding my breath, waiting for Kirsten to answer me.

"No, it wasn't like an admission. It was like a generic 'I'm sorry' type of thing. So I politely said thank you. And then he went into a spiel about how he doesn't blame Tim for helping out the authorities, and that he doesn't hold any ill will toward him, and a whole bunch of other crap. I just sat there and listened to him until I brought up his sister's name. And when he acted like she could not have had anything to do with his murder, that's when I went off the deep end and let him have it."

"I know that he didn't like that."

"Of course, he didn't. But I didn't hold back any punches and he hung up on me."

I burst into laughter. "Did he really?"

"Yes, he did."

"That coward," I commented, and shook my head. "So, does Alayna know anything about Tim's funeral service?"

"Nope. This service is strictly for family and close friends. But if she happens to find out about it and shows up, which I highly doubt, I will make her regret the day she was ever born."

I cracked a huge smile. "I'm sure you will," I said.

I have to admit that I would love to see Kirsten and Alayna in action. That would do more than make my day. It would make my entire year. So I might have to do some backdoor shenanigans to make that happen. Who knew? I might be able to get Kirsten and Alayna to fight. That would be the ultimate get-back against Alayna, especially with all the shit she had said to my face and behind my back to Kirsten. So, what better way to pay her back for her insults?

Kirsten and I talked for a little more. I thought that she was going to ask to pay another visit into Tim's office, but the request never came up. Instead, she said goodbye and made her exit. I stood there and watched her as she drove away and wondered if she really believed me when I told her that Alayna was lying about Tim and me? If she didn't, she sure made me believe otherwise.

When I got off work the following morning, around 8:00 a.m., I got in my car and drove over to Alayna's house. I made sure that when I drove into the neighborhood, I didn't stand out. Thankfully, no one was out and about, so I was able to park my car, get out of it, and mosey my way up to Alayna's house without being seen. I took a Xerox copy of the business card I got from Kirsten the day before, placed it in the crack of Alayna's front door, and eased back off the front porch before being seen by her. Now I couldn't say for sure if one of the nosey neighbors saw me, but I was sure that I had evaded Alayna. And that was the plan. Now let's see if she would show up to this funeral. I would wait with bated breath.

CHAPTER 25

Alayna

I WANTED TO MAKE A LUNCH RUN, SINCE I HAD NOTHING IN MY RE-frigerator to eat. I figured a bowl of Chipotle would be fitting today, so I slipped on sweats, socks, and a pair of sneakers. Then I grabbed my purse and car keys and headed toward the front door. As I pulled the front door open, I noticed a sticky-note-size white piece of paper floating around in the air until it fell down to the floor of the porch. I reached down and picked it up. When I looked down at the faint piece of paper, I realized that it was a photocopy of a business card. And the business card was from Aldridge Family Cemetery in Virginia Beach. At the bottom of the card was the time and date of Tim's funeral.

My heart instantly dropped into the pit of my stomach. So I looked up from the piece of paper and peered around at my immediate surroundings to see if someone was standing around watching me. But after scanning the area as far as my eyes would go, no one or nothing stuck out to me. So I wondered who could've left a copy of this business card here? And then I wondered if this was an invitation? I also wondered if I should go? Damn, I wished that I had the answers to those questions, because I would be in a better place mentally.

While trying to figure out who could've left this card here, I instantly lost my appetite and found myself stepping back into the house and closing the door behind me. With the business card in hand, I grabbed my cell phone from my handbag and called Pricilla. She didn't answer the first time, so I called her right back. Thankfully, she answered the second time I called.

"Hello," she answered after the second ring.

I sat down on the sofa and laid my head against the headrest. "Girl, you aren't gonna believe it."

"What has happened now?"

"I was leaving to go outside my house a few minutes ago, and when I opened the door, I found a copy of a business card to a funeral home in Virginia Beach, and it had Tim's funeral service time and date on it. So somebody left it there for me to find it. But I'm confused as to why they didn't knock on my door and give it to me?"

"Who do you think left it?" Pricilla threw the question back at me.

"See, that's the thing . . . I don't know."

"Think it was Tim's wife?"

"She knows that I fucked her husband. So I know it wasn't her."

"Then maybe one of the Feds left it there, to get a reaction out of you? They'll do anything to rattle your cage. I mean, look at how they harassed Zo at the jail."

"Now that you mentioned it, it probably was them. And if it was, then that would be a very cruel joke."

"Yeah, it would. So, what are you going to do?"

"What do you mean?" I asked her. I wanted clarity.

"Are you going to the funeral?"

"Of course not. And set myself up to be questioned about what happened that night? And not only that, his family is going to look at me like I'm crazy for showing up to his funeral. It wouldn't surprise me if his wife and kids try to attack me on sight."

150

"Now they'll probably try to question you, but I doubt it if they'd try to put hands on you."

"Shit, you never know with white people. They play by a different set of rules," I pointed out.

"Yeah, you got a point there," Pricilla agreed. "So, what are you going to do?"

"I'm not gonna do shit but sit my ass at home."

"Good idea. Stay away from anyone connected to Tim."

"I wonder if the guys at the station are going to the funeral?"

"Of course, they are."

"I wonder what they're going to say when they don't see me show up?"

"Who cares? If there were a different set of circumstances, then you could go. But it's not like that, you gotta sit this one out," Pricilla insisted, and she was right.

I mean, as bad as I wanted to see Tim's rat ass before he was put in the ground, it couldn't happen. So maybe I'd see him in the afterlife. And then maybe I wouldn't. I hoped that he made things right with God. Because if he didn't, he'd gotten a one-way trip to hell. And from what I heard, that place is hot. So, if that was where he was going, he'd better dress for the extreme heat. Fucking snitch!

CHAPTER 26

Kirsten

*I*COULDN'T BELIEVE THAT I WAS LOOKING AT THE CASKET WITH MY husband lying inside of it. It seemed like it was just yesterday when he said we were going to spend this Christmas in the Bahamas. We had everything all planned out. It was supposed to be a surprise for the kids and now it was an afterthought. Who would've thought that I would be burying my husband at this stage in my life? As I looked at my kids standing next to me in tears, it hurt my soul to know they wouldn't ever be able to hold their father again and tell him that they loved him. T.J. wouldn't be able to go fishing with him anymore, and Baby Girl wouldn't be able to have him walk her down the aisle on her wedding day. What a sad occasion.

As the priest delivered the eulogy, I gazed around at the small crowd gathered around my husband's casket and I saw the familiar faces of family, childhood friends, a few of our neighbors, and the firefighters who worked with him. It brought me so much joy to see these people standing here with me at a time like this. They made me feel as though I wasn't alone, that they were going to be by my family's side during this tragic ordeal, and I was eternally grateful.

The service came to an end, with the priest saying a prayer and then dismissing the small crowd. Before everyone left, they made their way by the kids and me and wished us farewell. After hugs and kisses were exchanged, they departed, and I stayed back with the kids and watched as the groundskeepers lowered Tim's casket into the ground. It was an unbearable sight. I cried a few tears, but for the most part, I wanted to be strong for the kids. They needed me now, more than ever.

"Think we're going to see Dad again in heaven?" my daughter asked me through tears.

The word "heaven" made me think of his murder all over again and I lost it. I began sobbing uncontrollably. The kids moved close to me in a huddle and cradled me with their embrace. We held each other tight, but in a comforting way.

"It's okay, Mommy. It's okay to cry," my daughter assured me.

I was floored at the level of maturity this young lady was showing me. I mean, I was supposed to be the one saying this. But no, my daughter and I had switched roles and she was handling the situation like a pro.

When we finally walked away from the grave site, I reassured my daughter that we would see their father again in heaven and her face lit up that instant. It seemed like the sun had parted the clouds. That was a great moment for me. But that dark cast that had followed me since Tim's death reappeared while I was getting into the backseat of the funeral home-issued limo. Before I hunched my back to get into the car, I saw a black figure in my peripheral vision. I looked to my right and saw someone wearing all black, standing near the five-foot-tall headstone that looked like a monument. I did a double take, and then when I refocused my eyes, that person was gone.

"Wait, wasn't someone just standing there?" I mumbled to myself. Was I seeing things? Or was my mind playing tricks on me? Either way, I was too drained to figure it out and got inside of the car.

As the driver drove us away from the cemetery, I got one last look at Tim's grave site and blew a kiss goodbye.

"Until the next time," I whispered.

CHAPTER 27

Jesse

I SAT ON THE PASSENGER SIDE OF PAUL'S PICKUP TRUCK, GAZING AT the landscape that made up the grounds of the cemetery. It was a sad affair watching everyone stand around Tim's casket, somber and heartbroken. Tim's kids really broke my heart. But what really stood out to me was that Alayna was a no-show. I knew without a doubt that she was going to show up to this funeral. But I was wrong. She didn't take the bait. Damn it! I thirsted for a good catfight between the wife and the mistress. What a show that would've been!

So, as I wallowed in my grief, knowing that I would never see Tim again, Paul interrupted my train of thought with a ridiculous question.

"I wonder if the jail officials would've allowed Alonzo to leave jail to come to Tim's funeral if someone had put in the request?"

I swear, that question seemed like it came out of left field.

"Of course not, silly. He's in there for killing three people," I pointed out.

Paul thought for a second. "You know what? I think you're right," he acknowledged. "How do you think the service was?"

"I think it was great. Very uplifting, considering the situation."

"You know, I thought that Alayna would've shown up."

"I really did too. But, then again, why show up to someone's funeral that you had killed?" I replied sarcastically.

"You don't know that for sure, Jesse."

"Oh, I know. And it's only a matter of time before everyone else will know too," I noted. In my assessment the story Alayna gave the homicide detectives didn't add up. There were too many loopholes. So, in my head, she still had some explaining to do.

As I thought about endless possibilities of what could've happened, I turned my attention to the funeral obituary program in my hand. I couldn't help but stare down at his photo. Kirsten had the funeral coordinator use Tim's fire chief portrait on the cover of the program. I admired the smile that he projected in the photo, which tugged at my heartstrings. I closed my eyes as tears drained from the sides of them. And when I opened them back up, I read the big, bold letters: **IN LOVING MEMORY OF TIM STANCIL. THE MAN WHO WORE THE WORLD ON HIS SHOULDERS: SUNRISE, AUGUST 8, 1974, TO SUNSET, OCTOBER 10, 2022.**

I suddenly felt like someone was screaming the words in my ears. The pain in my head increased and my heart pumped painfully in my chest. For a minute I thought I was about to have a heart attack as my eyes traveled down the text of the front page of the program.

Unconsciously I blinked a few times, not wanting to process what I was seeing, but it was there. Clear as day. I scanned the picture with my eyes. Searching for some sense of peace, but there was none. I couldn't see past the sparkle in Tim's eyes. It was magnetic. And I found myself not being able to stop staring at his face. From there my emotions started taking over me so much that the tears started stinging in the backs of my eye sockets. I hung my head low and said nothing, and that's when Paul noticed my mood had changed.

"Hey, Jess, you all right?" he asked me with a look of concern.

I looked up and assured him that I was. But the tears in my eyes told a different story.

"Are you sure?" he pressed.

I wiped the side of my eyes with my hands and held my head back with hopes that it would hold back the rest of my tears. "Yes," I told him.

As bad as I wanted to tell him what Tim meant to me, and how bad I was going to miss him, I couldn't. Paul wouldn't understand. And then on top of that, he might not have believed me. So I left well enough alone, dried away the rest of my tears, and sobered up. This was the only thing left for me to do.

CHAPTER 28

Alonzo

ALAYNA AND PRICILLA WERE SITTING PATIENTLY ON THE OTHER side of the glass partition, waiting for me to enter from the opposite side just so I could get a look at their pretty faces. Our eyes connected when the CO escorted me in. You should've seen Pricilla's face light up. Alayna, on the other hand, smiled. But it wasn't one of those joyful smiles. It was a smile that was forced to create a façade.

After the CO uncuffed me, I sat down and picked up the phone from the wall that separated us. Since Pricilla had the phone in her hand, I spoke to her first. "What's up, baby?"

Her smile grew four more inches in diameter. "Missing you," she told me.

I smiled back. "I miss you too. Y'all all right?" I turned my attention from Pricilla to Alayna. Alayna's smile brightened.

"Yeah, we're good. I took her by Tim's grave site yesterday after the funeral was over."

"Oh, yeah, I did hear on the news that his funeral was yesterday. I was going to call y'all, but the phones were down all day. They just started working again this morning."

"I wondered why you hadn't called."

"Yeah, that was it," I told her. "Let me holla at my sister for a minute," I instructed her.

"Okay, hold on," Pricilla replied, and handed the phone to Alayna.

Alayna grabbed it and placed it against her ear. "What's up, big guy?" She kept smiling.

"What's up with all these smiles?"

"They say it's better to smile than to cry."

"That depends on who said it," I commented.

"You may have a point there," she said.

"So you went to Tim's funeral?" I got straight to the point.

"No, I waited until the service was over and then visited his grave site."

"How did it make you feel?" She and I knew what she did. But Pricilla didn't know. So, because this was a secret between us, I had to make sure that I asked her the question without Pricilla actually knowing what I was talking about.

"What do you mean?" she seemed puzzled.

"What was going through your mind while you were standing there?"

"Nothing, really," she started off saying. But I could tell she was unsure as to how to answer my question. It seemed as if she didn't want to look vulnerable. Or maybe she was feeling remorse and didn't want to tell me. But I wasn't letting her off that easy.

"Do you miss him?" I probed.

She hesitated and then she said, "Kinda."

I smiled. "Okay, now I see that we're getting somewhere."

"I only went out there to get some stuff off my chest," she said. I could tell that she was building up the courage to express her true feelings. "I stood there and told him how I felt about everything. I told him how I felt about how things ended with us. And then I ended the conversation by saying, 'I'm sorry that things happened the way that they did.'"

158

"Is that all you said?" I pressed. It seemed like she was holding back because Pricilla was sitting there next to her.

"Yeah, that's all I said," she insisted. But Pricilla disagreed and took the phone out of her hand.

"Baby, that's a lie. You should've heard her screaming at his grave. I was sitting in my car, and I heard her yelling like she was mad at the world," Pricilla noted, and then she handed the phone back to Alayna.

I looked back at Alayna and shook my head and gave her a half smile. In my head I was laughing, because I could only imagine what that conversation was like. I could see the aggression right now, through her stoic little facial expression. And she knew that I saw it too, that's why she smiled.

"So you had a lot to say to him, huh?" I poked fun at her, wanting her to loosen up a bit, even though I knew that right now wasn't the best time to talk about this. She and I would have our time to discuss this situation more fully when Pricilla wasn't around.

She smiled at me again. "Can we talk about something else? Like what's going on with your case?" Alayna changed the subject.

"Well, my attorney filed the motion . . ." I began to say, but Alayna cut me off in midsentence.

"What kind of motion?"

"It's a motion to suppress evidence. And if we can prove that the evidence the prosecutor has is faulty, then the judge has no choice but to throw the case out."

Alayna became overjoyed. "That's fucking good news, Zo!"

I could see Pricilla getting antsy on the other side of the partition. I could tell that she wanted to hear what I was saying. "Tell her what I just said about the motion and what it would do for me," I instructed.

I watched as Alayna reiterated the news, and then I watched the excitement on Pricilla's face after she got the news. She lit up like a Christmas tree. She immediately grabbed the phone from Alayna's hands again.

"So this is a sure thing?" she wanted to know.

"If it goes like my attorney says it should go, then I'm going to be coming home, baby," I replied confidently.

Pricilla started jumping around in her seat. "Calm down, baby! Now it hasn't happened yet," I had to remind her. "Ask Alayna, have those homicide detectives tried to talk to her again after she went down there with her lawyer?"

"I'ma let you ask her," Pricilla insisted, and handed the telephone back to Alayna.

Alayna took the phone back. "What did you say?"

"I asked her if those cops ever came back to harass you about Tim's murder?"

"Nope. I haven't heard from them. But I know that they're watching me like a hawk and hoping I may somehow slip up and lead them to the killer. I mean, you've watched TV. Cops will do anything to solve their cases. It wouldn't surprise me if my phones are tapped, and my car has a tracker on it."

That possibility struck my thoughts. "Yeah, it wouldn't surprise me either," I agreed with her.

She was right, cops will do anything to move a case along. I mean, look at my situation. The Feds were pulling out all the stops to lock this case down. But their overconfidence and lack of preparation and protection for their witnesses had stonewalled their whole investigation. Now who was looking crazy in the face?

"But just be careful. Because the fact that those detectives know they don't have anything on you, they could get desperate and try to plant some DNA evidence on you. So keep your eyes and ears open," I advised.

"Don't worry, I will."

CHAPTER 29

Alayna

ONE MONTH LATER, AND TODAY WAS THE DAY. IT WAS TIME TO head to court. This was Alonzo's first court appearance, and we were having his motion of discovery heard today. Pricilla and I were on pins and needles the entire drive to the federal court building. We prayed before we left the house and we prayed before we exited the car.

"Ready?" I asked her.

"As ready as I'll ever be," she replied.

"Well, let's do this," I encouraged her, and we both closed the car doors and stepped onto the curb.

As soon as we made our way down the sidewalk and up the stairs of the federal court building, I heard loud voices erupt behind her. Chaotic and loud, to say the least. Annoyed, I turned around slowly to scold whoever was making the noise. I immediately caught a sharp pain in my side after I saw what was coming behind me. It was as if a never-ending line of people was rushing at me. My head whipped from side to side so fast, my eyes couldn't keep up with it. "What is going on here?" I belted out.

Finally, when the crowd stopped in front of me, I realized they were reporters. My nostrils flared up instantly as I looked at the gaggle of scavengers that surrounded me.

"Alayna, did your brother kill those people?" one reporter asked.

"Yeah, Alayna, is your brother guilty of all charges?" another reporter asked.

"What about the insurance fraud charges? Did he really take those people for all of that money?" another reporter shouted among the chaos.

I felt like I was under fire. I wasn't about to stand there and answer all these questions, so I turned around and bolted for the front entrance of the federal building. Pricilla followed me.

After we got inside, we stopped to go through the metal detector, and once we were cleared by the U.S. Marshals, we proceeded onto the next hallway. Then we stopped to take a breather.

"What the fuck was that all about?" Pricilla spoke first.

"What if the judge hears everything and sends this thing to trial?" Pricilla became worried.

"He won't. We have this in the bag. There are no witnesses, Pricilla, and the people who Zo and Tim took money from aren't willing to come forward and testify."

"But what if they changed their minds and they are here today?" she asked, her face folded into a frown.

"It wouldn't matter because the reports are in Tim's name. Not Zo's. And do you think that the government is going to pursue an insurance fraud case against a dead man?"

Pricilla thought for a moment and then she said, "I guess you have a point there." And then she smiled.

"Look, everything will work out," I said with a suddenly cheery voice coming out of my mouth and followed it with a phony smile. It was the role I played for so long that it just came second nature to me.

Act as if this bad thing is really not happening. This is the way my fa-

ther taught me how to be when we had to break the news to the families that they had lost loved ones, or their loved ones were in bad shape, but we had resources that would help them rebuild their lives. It's all bull-shit!

"Come on, let's get into this courtroom," I instructed her.

As we began to walk in the direction of the courtroom, I saw the U.S. attorney, Agent McGee, and Agent Fletcher walking alongside Jesse, the fucking firefighter. Now what the hell was he doing here?

He stood there with a snide grin on his face. "Hello, Alayna," he had the nerve to say.

I swear, I wanted to slap the fuck out of him. So, after I screamed silently in my head, my cheeks flushed red, and my nostrils flared instantly.

"What are you doing here?" I huffed after I stormed toward him with my eyes squinted into dashes.

Pricilla was hot on my tail. She tried to restrain me. "Come on now, Alayna, he's not worth it."

"Oh, I'm definitely worth it, especially after I give my testimony today," he stated cruelly.

"You don't know shit," I snorted sardonically as my hands involuntarily curled into fists.

"I know enough." He didn't back down and then he chuckled. "And even if I didn't, I would lie first before I let your brother walk away a free man," he threatened.

My eyebrows shot up into arches on my face. "Try it!" I dared him.

At that point I immediately wanted to punch Jesse in his face, but Pricilla grabbed my arm gently and calmly pulled it back. I eyed Jesse like he posed no threat. He didn't even flinch. He eyed me back evilly and I returned the gaze. Both of us held our ground for a few tense seconds.

"All right, you two, break it up," Agent McGee instructed as she stood between us like a referee.

"You better get him before I do," I threatened.

"I'd like to see it," he dared me once again.

This guy was really showing off in front of the Feds. I swear, everything inside of me wished that I would've had K-Rock and his homeboy get rid of this fucking asshole. Shut his mouth up, once and for all.

"Come on, Pricilla, this idiot isn't worth it."

"I'm going to prove you wrong," he said, and then he walked off.

I shot him an evil look and shook my head in utter disgust, because I wanted to run down behind him and rip his fucking head off. How dare this guy continue to run his mouth like this? His voice truly irritated me. Someone needed to shut him up.

Pricilla saw how my body was beginning to tremble, so she grabbed and pulled me in the opposite direction of Jesse. She ended up pulling me in the direction of the courtroom. She figured that the farther I got away from him, the quicker I could cool down.

So, as we drew near the courtroom door, it opened, and I immediately gasped, swallowing the lump of fear that had formed in the back of my throat. Was I really seeing things? Was I really looking at K-Rock coming toward us? I looked at Pricilla.

"What is he doing here?" I asked her.

"I told him to come here and show Alonzo some support. We need to show the judge that Alonzo has family who loves and supports him," Pricilla explained.

"But K-Rock isn't his family. He's your family," I huffed. I was pissed. I mean, why would she ask this guy to come here? I couldn't let any of these people lay eyes on him. This stupid motherfucker could become a suspect and then my whole cover would be blown if that happened.

"What's good, fam?" He smiled as he greeted us.

Pricilla leaned in and hugged him. He leaned in and hugged me next, so I leaned in very quickly, reached my arms around him, tapped my hands on his back, and whispered to him that being here wasn't a good idea. When I pulled back from him, he parted a nervous smile and shot a sharp look at Pricilla, indicating that it was her idea. But that wasn't good enough for me. He knew we had made a pact for him not to ever come around me, at least until this thing had died down. But no, he had to listen to his dumb-ass sister and agree to come to my brother's trial when all the fucking federal investigators would be here. What was he thinking?

"How are you, Mrs. Curry?" a voice greeted me from my left side. I turned around toward the voice. I was so lost in what was going on with K-Rock that I had not realized Detective Showers and his partner, Pittman, were talking to me until they had come within inches of me.

I furrowed my eyebrows and looked at the ugly-faced men like they were pieces of garbage, and I asked myself, why were they here? This wasn't their case. So, why meddle in my brother's business? It wouldn't surprise me if they were working with the Feds, trying to tie both cases together, since they couldn't get a confession out of me.

"What are they doing here?" Pricilla whispered.

I ignored her question and kept my focus on them. "I'm fine, and you?" I replied to the detectives, trying to act as if their presence didn't at all bother me. But it did.

I mean, look at who was standing in front of us? The person who should be their number one fucking suspect. The very person who wasn't supposed to be here. The very person I told to stay his ass out of sight. But no, the one day he decided to show up, so did the detectives, who didn't know it yet, but were looking for him. What a fucking disaster!

"Oh, we're great. Just coming here to check things out," Detective Showers noted, and smiled.

"I'm sure you are," I commented sarcastically. I turned my back on them. "Don't look nervous now," I mumbled so that only K-Rock could hear me.

"I'm good," he tried to assure me, but I saw right through his painted-on facial façade.

"Well, after today, maybe not so much," I pointed out. Because I wanted him to know that he screwed up royally. Not only were the Feds looking at everyone who came here in support of my brother, Zo, but the freaking detectives who were investigating Tim's murder were here and were looking for anyone connected to me and my brother. This could not have been a more screwed-up time for me and this nitwit standing next to me.

"Come on, let's go inside this courtroom and get a seat," Pricilla suggested, and grabbed my hand. Before I took the first step in the direction of the courtroom, I looked at K-Rock and whispered, "You can't stay here. Leave!"

K-Rock stood there clueless for a second and then he perked up and rushed to the right side of his sister, Pricilla. He grabbed her arm and leaned into her ear. He whispered something to her and she stopped walking. I stopped alongside of her and pretended not to know what was going on.

"Really?" she whispered back to him.

"Yeah, but if you get a chance to talk to him, tell him I was here and that I'm rooting for him," K-Rock added.

"Okay," Pricilla said, unsure if that was really what she wanted to say.

"All right, Alayna, y'all keep your head up," K-Rock said, and then he walked off.

"Where is he going?" I asked.

"He said something about how he's not feeling all these Feds and that he had to get out of here."

"I would also feel that way if I sold drugs in the hood."

"My brother doesn't sell drugs!" she barked.

"Well, he's doing something illegal," I barked back, and then I yanked her arm and led her down the hall toward the courtroom.

WHERE THERE'S SMOKE

When Pricilla and I entered the courtroom, I saw some of the victims' family members lined up in the row of seats, along with friends, bystanders, and a few local news reporters sitting around as well. Sitting at the front of the courtroom were the U.S. attorney, the U.S. Marshals, and federal agents. Standing off to the side were the homicide detectives from the Chesapeake Police Department. And to just see them all posing around got me to thinking that if only I could get all of them in that one room, with paperwork in hand, and blow that damn thing up to smithereens. What a great day that would be! And my brother could be home free. Wishful thinking, though. Because on some real shit, I saw the lawyer was going to have to do his job and beat this thing. Aside from that, all we could do was hope and pray.

CHAPTER 30

Alonzo

I WALKED INTO THE COURTROOM, AND CRAMPS INVADED MY STOMach like a rogue army. I sat next to my attorney—with confidence that I was going to walk out of here today.

"All rise for the Honorable Tom Matthews," the courtroom deputy instructed everyone in attendance.

My heart was hammering against my chest as the gray-haired old judge stepped out of his chambers and onto his throne. I kept my eyes on him from the time he sat down. The courtroom was pin-drop quiet and packed to full capacity.

"You may be seated," the judge instructed us.

"Your Honor, this is case 593019, *the United States* versus *Riddick . . .*" the courtroom deputy stated.

"Thank you, Bob," Judge Matthews said; then he turned his attention toward me and my attorney. He even looked over at the U.S. attorney, who was shuffling papers around in front of him. Then he glanced down at the court documents placed in front of him. He sifted through the first several pages and then looked up.

"Okay, here is my position on this case . . . After looking at all the evidence presented by the U.S. attorney, it has become apparent that there isn't enough here to move forward. So I am dismissing all charges against Mr. Riddick," he declared.

My eyes popped open in utter shock, and I almost jumped up from my seat while the courtroom erupted into pandemonium. There were screams and moans.

A few of the family members cried out, "What?!"

I heard a woman's voice screech, "Are you out of your mind?"

"No way! That can't be," I heard someone else say.

"Order!" the judge shouted, banging his gavel. Silence came once again. But I could feel the evil eyes from the courtroom crowd bearing down on me.

In the meantime, two reporters ran out of the courtroom so they could be the first to break the news. I turned around and looked at Pricilla and then at Alayna and smiled at them both. Pricilla and Alayna were both ecstatic. The joy on their faces was priceless.

"Face the judge, he's not done talking," Swartz whispered as he poked me in my arm.

"Aww . . . man, I can't believe that I'm going home. We did it! You did it!" I whispered back.

I sat there in my chair and listened to the judge's final words. After he addressed the family of my victims and then me, he exited the courtroom. I could honestly say that this was the best day of my entire life. It could never get better than this.

I know that I am a free man now, but it's still kind of unreal to know I'm getting out of this hellhole today. Hearing the judge tell me that the investigators didn't have enough evidence against me to proceed with the murder cases, and then to dismiss all my charges, it was an all-around victory. My sister, Alayna, and my attorney came through for me and now I was a fucking free man!

The prosecutor acted like he wanted to rip the judge's freaking head off and all I could do was smile. The reaction in the courtroom was priceless. It was like something off of Court TV. I stood there in amazement. I felt untouchable now.

As I entered back into the cell block, I was greeted by a few niggas I started kicking it with after I vetted everyone in this block. My cellmate approached me first.

"You good?" he asked.

I smiled and postured myself to shake his hand. "Yeah, man, I'm more than good. I'm great," I assured him and gave him a hand dap and half of an embrace, ending it with a pat on the back.

He smiled back. "Going home?"

I burst into excitement. "You fucking right! I'm getting the hell out of here!" My voice echoed through the block.

"When? Now?"

"As soon as they process it."

"No fucking way?! How did you pull that off?" my cellmate replied with astonishment.

"The prosecutor couldn't produce the evidence to move forward with the case, so the judge dismissed all my charges," I explained as we stood in the middle of the cell block floor. There were a few bystanders listening to my conversation with my cellmate as they hung outside the door of their cell or sat around the benches, pretending to be watching television. I even saw a nigga walk over to the phone, pick it up, and pretend to talk to someone just so he could hear my conversation more clearly. I swear, the niggas in here were nosier than women.

"That's fucking dope! I'm happy for you, man!" my cellie insisted.

"So you're leaving?" I heard a voice say from behind. I looked over my shoulders and saw Roman walking from the opposite end of the cell block, so I turned around to greet him.

I leaned in and gave him a hand dap after he came within arm's distance of me. "The judge let me go," I said modestly.

When you're in this environment, you can't be too cocky

when you announce that you're getting out of jail. The guys who have been locked up for a long time, or were waiting to go to trial, envy the other inmates who get to go home before them. It could become a dangerous situation for a weak man who's on his way out the door. So you got to be careful not to brag.

"So you beat the charges?" Roman asked. He seemed confused and needed clarity.

"Yeah, the prosecutor failed to provide the judge with the evidence needed to move forward, so the judge dismissed all my charges," I replied candidly.

"Oh, damn! Some niggas have all the luck!" Roman commented with a half-smile. I couldn't tell if he was happy for me or if he was sad that I was leaving. I was starting to get confused.

"That wasn't luck. That was a sum of fifty grand in attorney's fees and a couple of lost witnesses," I joked.

My cellmate burst into laughter. "That'll do it every time," Wayne commented.

"Nigga, I thought you said that you were innocent?" Roman wondered aloud.

"Always remember, it isn't what you do, it's what you can prove." I leaned in toward his ear and whispered so that only he and I could hear it.

Roman pulled back from me and gave me this dark look. It was almost menacing in a way. So I had to step back and look at him for a second, but I kept my mouth closed and waited for him to speak. I wanted to see where his head was. But I could tell immediately that he noticed how I was looking at him and dialed back his body language, and he even fixed his facial expression before he opened his mouth. I stood there patiently.

"I'm happy for you, bro. It's a good feeling when you see niggas leave out this muthafucka! But you got to be careful when you say certain shit like, 'It ain't what you do, it's what you can prove,' when it comes to a murder rap."

"What's wrong with saying that?" I wondered aloud.

171

"You never know who's listening," he told me.

And once he uttered those words, I stood there and realized there was some truth to his statement. But then again, this situation didn't apply to me, because my claim wouldn't come back and bite me in the ass, especially when you couldn't bring my witnesses back from the dead. It was highly impossible. So I threw caution to the wind and let that shit he said roll off my back.

"Yeah, you're right, but in this case that shit doesn't apply," I added. It was as simple as that.

Taken aback by my comment, Roman chuckled mischievously and, in the iconic words of Denzel Washington, said, "My man . . ." Seconds later, he walked off.

My cellmate and I watched Roman as he walked back to his cell. I shrugged off the nigga's antics and proceeded to my cell. It was time for me to pack up my shit so I could get the hell out of here when the CO called my name to be released.

Inside the cell Wayne pointed out Roman's behavior. "I thought you and that nigga was cool?" he asked as he stood by the entryway of the cell, watching as I began to pack up my things. He would periodically look over his shoulders to make sure no one was close enough to our cell to listen to our conversation.

"I thought we were cool too. But he's acting like he's not too happy that I'm going home," I pointed out.

"Yeah, he's on some real hating shit, right now."

"He can be on whatever he wants, just as long as he keeps that shit down on his end of the cell block," I stated, and I meant every word.

"He's probably mad because he's losing a chess mate," my cellie joked.

"Well, I'm sorry to hear that. But it's time for me to go. Maybe somebody else will come rolling through here and will sit down and play a few games with him, but I'm just not that guy anymore. I've got things to do, places to go, and pussy to fuck when I get home."

My cellie chuckled. "I'm with you . . ." Wayne commented, and then he looked on.

Four long hours had passed, the shift had changed, and my name still hadn't been called. In two and a half more hours, it would be lockdown and I wasn't trying to spend another night in this place. Fuck no!

So I yelled for the CO. It took almost ten minutes for the redneck cracker to show up at the bars.

His name was Bobby Wright. He was a rookie, but he had a lot of family members who worked throughout the jail, so he walked around like he ran shit.

"Whatcha want, inmate?" he asked as he stood on the other side of the cell bars. This guy was six-three and every bit of 275 pounds. He was a big guy. Your real-life orange-colored hair, with matching-colored eyebrows, mustache, and beard—as hillbilly as they came.

"Why hasn't anyone called me to leave this joint yet? I went to court today and the judge dismissed all my charges," I explained.

"Yeah, I heard about that. Lucky you!" he commented.

"Why is everybody saying that?"

"Saying what?"

"Lucky me!"

"Because you are lucky. Who commits murder and then gets away with it?"

"I didn't kill those people. And the judge knew it too—that's why he set me free."

"Well, you ain't free yet."

"I will be, just as soon as you find out why it's taking your coworkers so long to process me out of this place."

"Hold your horses. They'll get to you."

"Can you find out how much longer it's going to be? I am not trying to stay here another night."

"They'll call me when they're ready for you," he said.

And I instantly got the impression that's what he meant. He wasn't about to call downstairs and find out why it was taking booking so long to call my name for release. As far as he was concerned, he was going home after this shift was over, so he couldn't care less about me.

"Yeah, a'ight," I said, and walked away from the cell bars. "Fucking lazy-ass cracker!" I mumbled. My words were barely audible.

"What did you say, inmate?"

"I ain't say shit," I replied.

I could see every eye turn in my direction. I wasn't about to give that CO any energy, especially since I was on my way out of the door.

Soon Roman peered his head out of his cell and called my name. I looked in his direction.

"What's up?"

"Wanna get into another game of chess before you leave?"

"Nah, I'm good."

"Come on, man, just this last one. Give me something to remember you by," he pressed.

I hesitated for a moment and then I said, "A'ight. Give me a minute."

"Come to my cell."

"You don't wanna play out in the dayroom?"

"Nah, come to my cell because I want to holla at you about something private."

"Yeah, a'ight. Be down there in a sec . . ." I told him after realizing that a game of chess would be something that could make my time go by, and before I would know it, the CO would be back calling my name.

I took a piss, grabbed a pack of chips from my bunk, and then

I made my way down to Roman's cell. He had the game set up on his mini desk when I entered his cell. He sat on his bottom bunk, and I sat on the metal chair mounted against his wall. He looked up and smiled at me. It was more like a smirk. Nevertheless, he was ready to play the game and so was I.

"You first," he started off.

I moved my first chess piece, and it was the pawn. And after I moved it, I watched the board as Roman moved the rook to the square across from him. Now it was my turn, so I moved my rook.

Immediately after I had done so, Roman opened dialogue. "How does it feel?"

"What do you mean?" I wondered as I moved my bishop, keeping my eyes on the board.

"About getting your charges dismissed?"

"It feels good as hell. There's no way in the world I could've stayed in prison for the rest of my life," I told him as I moved another one of my chess pieces.

"'If you do the crime, you gotta do the time.' I mean, ain't that what they say?" Roman said mechanically. His voice had changed all of a sudden and that prompted me to look up at him.

"But I didn't do it," I lied. But I knew Roman knew better.

"But you did . . ." he said, and his face turned cold. His eyes seemed glasslike.

Feeling uneasy about his immediate change in behavior, I stood up, and without notice, Roman's right hand grabbed a handful of fabric from the waist area of my jumpsuit and lunged a homemade shank into my stomach with his left hand. That blade penetrated me within a split second. I bellowed in agony as the pain engulfed me. I had nowhere to go but to the floor and I landed on my back.

Roman crawled on top of me and started stabbing me repeatedly. "You thought you were gonna get away with murder, didn't you? You fucking piece of shit! Those were my folks you killed, nigga, and you think that you were going to leave out of here alive. Not on my fucking watch, you piece of fucking scum!" he whispered demonically into my ears as he took the life out of me.

I couldn't do anything to fight back. I was losing lots of blood and I had no energy. I was dying and there was nothing anyone could do to save me. He was right. I wasn't leaving this place alive.

"Why did you wait . . . all . . . this . . . time to . . . kill me?" I managed to say as the blood began to drown me.

"Because that's all I had. I wanted to watch you and study you. Make sure I had the right guy, and you proved that to me when you acted like you had no sympathy for the old folks when the news started running stories on 'em. You always turned your back on the TV and said, 'Aww, fuck those old people. Ain't nobody kill them. They had one foot in the grave already,'" he reminded me.

By this time he had stopped plunging the blade inside of me. He had taken the shank out and watched the pool of blood escape my body while he reminded me of everything I did and said over the days leading up to this moment.

"I would tell you to tell my parents I love them and that I did this for them, but where you're going, you won't see them to give them that message," he added, and then he stuck me one last time.

Boom!

And just like that . . . everything around me went dark. I had no time to think about my fiancée or my sister. It was too late.

My soul was leaving my body.

Though I guess you could argue, my soul had left my body a long time ago, after my first insurance fraud and all my other horrendous crimes that followed.

If you enjoyed *Where There's Smoke*, you will love this sneak peek at Kiki Swinson's newest thriller, *Amber Alert*

PROLOGUE

"*G*ET THE FUCK OFF OF ME! YOU PIECE OF SHIT!" I BARKED AT him; my anger was starting to well up like a volcano.

I hadn't realized that I had spit at him until I saw a hunk of my DNA dangling from his face. He immediately wiped the spit from his face and examined it in his hand. It all seemed like everything was going in slow motion, because after he took his eyes off his hand, he looked at me and I could instantly see that his pupils were changing size rapidly. His previous calm face eased into a sinister frown. He raised a closed fist and lunged right at me. I saw it coming and I tried to duck, but it was too late.

"Aggh!" I shrieked.

Instinctively my hands flew up to my head in an attempt to stop him, but the blow plowed me smack-dab in the right side of my head. The impact took me out and I hit the floor hard.

Boom!

My insides felt like they had been knocked out of place and I was dazed.

"You fucking bitch!" I heard him say while I was trying to stop my head from spinning. "Spitting on me? Are you fucking crazy?

After all I've done for you? And that's how you repay me?" he grunted out the words as he loomed over me.

"You took my kids from me," I mustered up the will to say as I fought through the pain in my head.

"Fuck your kids!" his voice boomed, and then he lunged at me. I braced myself because I knew exactly what was coming next.

Boom!

"You fucking bitch!" he roared, and reached down and grabbed a fistful of my hair and wrapped it around his hand. He lifted my head off the floor and pulled it back down with brute force. The back of my head crashed to the floor with so much impact, I thought my brain would shoot through the front and burst out through my forehead.

I now knew what people meant when they got hit and said they were literally seeing stars. Flashes of psychedelic lights invaded my eyesight for at least thirty seconds. I was dazed and confused, and the pain was like nothing I'd ever felt before.

"Please stop! You're hurting me!" I cried out, trying to pry his fingers from my hair, but he wasn't relenting.

"Shut up, bitch! You're gonna take this ass kicking tonight," he growled while digging his fingers into my scalp, clutching my hair at the root, filling his palm up with it, and then dragging me across the floor.

Suddenly an excruciating pain shot through my scalp and radiated over my entire head. I swear, I had never felt pain like that in my head. It felt like my entire scalp was being ripped off. I started kicking and screaming.

"Please let me go. Let my fucking hair go," I yelled and screamed. Then I kicked at him again. This time my foot landed near his groin area. He flinched for a second, but the pain didn't last long at all, and he was back on me. This time he lunged at me with his face. My face was scrunched up and my eyes rolled into the back of my head. The impact felt like he rattled every organ in my body. Sweat immediately began pouring from every pore on my body.

I gagged, but nothing came up from my stomach. I was in so much pain, I felt like even the organs inside of my body hurt. My heart pounded painfully against my weakened chest bones and my stomach literally churned. I was wishing for death, because even that had to be better than what I was feeling at that moment.

"Leave my mommy alone!"

I heard a voice shout from the other side of the room. Instantaneously we both looked in that direction and saw my son pointing a gun directly at us. At that very moment I realized that the gun I was carrying on my waist had fallen out, onto the floor. And now my son had it in his small hand. My attacker didn't know this, but my son knew how to use and fire a gun properly. I had been teaching him how to hold and fire a gun since he was six years old. And right now he was looking very much like my savior.

"Hey, you better stop waving that gun around before you hurt somebody," Nick warned him as he stood straight up and started walking toward him.

"Leave my son alone!" I shouted as I began to pull myself up from the floor.

"Your son better put that gun away before I take it from him," he warned me as he continued toward Little Kevin.

I couldn't get up fast enough to get to this man before he grabbed a hold of my son. The adrenaline pumping inside of me became overwhelming as I scrambled in the direction of Nick and my son. My only thoughts were to get to my son before he did, but it seemed like I was moving in slow motion. And before I knew it, I saw Nick towering over my son as he stood there nervously with the gun pointed directly at him. Without a moment's notice, he lunged at my son, and then I heard the gun go off twice.

Pop! Pop!

CHAPTER 1

Ava

"*T*IME TO GET UP!" I SHOUTED FROM THE HALLWAY OUTSIDE OF my bedroom.

It was six-thirty on a Tuesday morning and it was time for the kids to get up and get ready for school. Getting resistance was something of the norm with my little kiddos. They hated getting out of bed in the morning to go to school, so I prepped myself for the push back.

I entered Little Kevin's room first, because he was the hardest to get out of bed. To my surprise he was already out of bed. I figured he was downstairs, probably eating a bowl of cereal or something, so I entered Kammy's bedroom next.

"It's time to get up, my darling," I said as I entered my baby girl's room. But just like Little Kevin, she wasn't in bed either. I knew then that she had gone downstairs with her brother to eat breakfast, so I made my way down to the kitchen to see what my little kiddos were into.

On my way I pictured cereal crumbs and spilled milk on the kitchen table, with the milk carton sitting a few inches away from the bowl, at room temperature, while Little Kevin and

183

Kammy were fighting over who got to look at the pictures on the cereal box. But when I turned the corner to the kitchen and saw that it was empty, I paused for a second and tried to collect my thoughts.

"Wait a minute," I mumbled, and then I turned in the opposite direction and called out their names. "Kammy! Little Kevin! Where are y'all?" I yelled out, loud enough so that they could hear me throughout the entire house. But I got no answer. So I called their names again.

"Kammy! Little Kevin! Where are you?" I shouted.

Paulina heard me calling the kids' names and appeared from her bedroom. She stood over the balcony of the hallway, dressed in her pajamas and robe, as she looked down at me in the living-room quarters of the house.

"Are the kids in the room with you?" I asked.

"No, they're not," she replied. "Have you checked the garage or outside?"

"I am now. But I want you to check the bathroom, all the closets, and underneath their beds, because it sounds like they're playing a game of hide-and-seek," I told her.

"They better not be . . ." Paulina said as her voice trailed off.

While Paulina searched upstairs, I started searching everywhere I could think that the kids could hide. First I went into the garage and then I exited the house through the side door, and when I realized that they weren't out there, I walked back into the house and searched all the closets, underneath all the tables, and still there was no sign of my children. This immediately became a cause for me to be alarmed, and I panicked.

"Paulina, did you find them yet?" I shouted from the living room.

Paulina appeared on the balcony. "No," she responded somberly.

"Oh, my God, Paulina, where are my kids?" I said helplessly. I was actually at a loss for words and I couldn't think straight either.

"I don't know, but they're not in the house, so they must be outside. Maybe the backyard?" Paulina suggested as she made her way downstairs.

I didn't wait for her. I raced back through the kitchen and headed toward the side door that led to my backyard. I heard Paulina in the distance, so I knew that she was behind me, but I kept going. Finding out where my kids were was eating me up inside. By the time I made it around the corner of my house, I heard Paulina scream. It startled the hell out of me, and I stopped in my tracks. When I turned around and saw that she wasn't behind me, I realized that the scream came from inside the house, so I ran back in that direction.

When I reentered my home, I saw Paulina standing in the kitchen, holding a note in her hand, so I ran toward her and snatched it from her. In bold letters the first words were: **DO NOT CALL THE COPS OR YOUR KIDS WILL DIE!** Reading those words, I instantly became sick, and I wanted to vomit. Instead, I continued to read on:

> *Your kids are safe and will be returned to you if you pay their $2 million-dollar ransom. You have seventy-two hours to come up with the money. If you don't, then you will never see your children again. And let me please remind you that you must not call the cops. If you do, your kids will die!*

"Oh, my God, Paulina, these people have my kids!" I screamed, and broke down into tears.

Paulina embraced me and held me tight. "Don't worry! We're gonna get them back." She tried to calm me.

"But what if we don't, Paulina? They're asking for two million dollars." I became doubtful.

"We gotta think positive. Now let's get Mr. Frost on the phone and he will come home, get the money together, and we can have our babies home by tonight." She handed me the cordless phone that was nearby on the island.

I dialed my husband's cell phone number and it rang five times and then he answered it.

"Hello," he said, sounding as if he had just woken up.

"Kevin!" I screamed through the phone.

Fear had penetrated my entire heart and placed a dark cloud over my head. It felt like I was drowning in heartache and confusion. I couldn't quite put my thoughts together either. It felt like I was losing all my senses.

"What's wrong?" he replied.

"The kids are gone. Someone took them," I added.

"What do you mean, 'someone took them'?" he wanted to know. My outburst alarmed him.

"Someone kidnapped them, Kevin." I began to cry.

"How do you know that?"

"Because they're not here and I'm holding a ransom note in my hand."

"What fucking ransom note?!" his voice screeched. "What does it say?"

"It says that they have our kids and if we want them back, we must come up with two million dollars. Right now they are fine, but if we call the cops, we will never see them again. Someone will get in touch with us very soon with drop-off instructions," I told him between sobs.

"Is that it?" he shouted through the phone.

"Yes, that's all that's in this letter."

"When did you find it?"

"After I searched the entire house for the kids."

"Where did you find the letter?"

"On the kitchen table."

"How long ago did you find the letter?"

"A few minutes ago."

"Wait, what time is it?" he asked as I began to hear him shuffling things around in the background.

"It's a little after seven a.m.," I managed to say.

"Where is Paulina?"

"She's right here, standing next to me."

"Did she stay there last night?"

"Yes."

"Did she hear anything?"

"She said she didn't."

"What time did you guys go to bed last night?"

"The kids lay down around ten o'clock. Paulina went to bed a little bit after that. And I probably dozed off around midnight." I continued to cry. Tears saturated my face.

"So that means that they were taken between midnight and just before dawn?" Kevin calculated aloud. This announcement hurt me to my heart and I screamed out in agony. "Noooooo! Don't say that," I cried out once more. The pain was becoming unbearable.

"Ava, this is not the time to break down. We've gotta stay strong and positive," he coached me.

"I know, Kevin, but those are my babies and we need to hurry up and get them back," I whined.

"And we will," he said, and then he fell silent for a couple of seconds. All you could hear were my sobs.

"This just doesn't make any sense. I mean, who could do this?" Kevin asked out loud.

"If I knew, I wouldn't be calling you," I replied sarcastically.

"And what is that supposed to mean?"

"You should've been here. If you were here, none of this would've happened. Our kids could probably be in bed right now as we speak. But no, you're always away from the house. Doing

God knows what, while I'm here taking care of the kids by my-self. And now look at the mess we're in. Someone has my fuck-ing kids and I don't know where they are or if they're all right!" I shouted through the phone.

I wanted Kevin to know that his presence at home could've prevented this from happening. He was the reason why the kids were gone.

"Look, Ava, just calm down and don't do anything until I get there. I'm hopping on the next plane out of Canada. I'll be home in a few hours," he assured me, and then he ended the call.

After that conversation I collapsed on the sofa and Paulina sat next to me. All I could think about was where my babies could be and who had them? Two million was a lot of freaking money. And with Kevin's flashy image and storefront businesses, it was easy to see why the kidnappers thought we had that kind of money. And it wouldn't be hard to believe that the kidnappers also knew that Kevin wasn't going to be home last night either.

See, he was on a business trip in Canada trying to secure an auto parts deal with a Canadian businessman. What Kevin does is sell luxury cars at a storefront location. He also has an auto parts store, which was why he was trying to secure the auto parts deal in Canada. This deal could make him a lot of money and potentially allow him to open a few more stores in the area. It could definitely be a franchise opportunity, something that he'd been wanting for a very long time.

Now I understood his work ethic, but when it took time away from the family, as it always did, that was when I had a problem. Don't get me wrong. He's a great provider and he's a good fa-ther, but the constant time away from home created this intense wedge and chaos wreaked havoc. But, hey, what could I say? I signed up for this when I said, "I do." So I gotta deal with the bullshit that came along with him.

"So, what did he say?" Paulina wanted to know.

"He said that he was going to get on the next flight out of Canada."

"So he's on his way back home?"

"He better be," I hissed, and wiped the tears from my eyes with the back of my hand.

Immediately after I ended the call with Kevin, I called my father. He was a seventy-one-year-old retiree who sat at home and watched television all day. He used to go on fishing trips, but since my mother came down with dementia, he generally never left the house, unless he had to go run errands. When I was not doing anything, I'd run the errands for him. My dad was a good man, and despite the chaotic lifestyle I used to live, he never judged me or disowned me. That was why I've never lied to him and kept him in the loop about everything that went on in my life. He was basically like my best friend, since I didn't have any siblings or close female friends.

Now I wrestled with the thought of telling him about the kids, because I didn't need him calling the cops. But I knew that I couldn't keep this type of information from him. I wouldn't be able to live with myself if something happened and I didn't get my babies back.

"Daddy, what took you so long to answer the phone?" I asked after he answered the phone on the fifth ring.

He started chuckling. "I was letting the nurse in when the phone started ringing."

"Is it the same nurse?" I wondered aloud.

"Yes, we still have Nancy. She's been good to us," he said joyfully. "So, what's up? Where are the kids?" My father changed the subject.

"Dad, I need you to come over." I became serious.

"Is there something wrong?" He seemed concerned.

"I can't talk about it over the phone," I said adamantly.

"Are the kids all right?" he pressed.

"No, they're not. Can you please come over?" I insisted, hoping he would take my direction.

"Okay, I'm on my way."

CHAPTER 2

Kevin

"*B*ABY, WHAT'S GOING ON?" TY ASKED ME AS SHE EASED HER WAY to my side of the bed, dressed in the fitted black lace lingerie piece I purchased for her the day before.

It was our third-year anniversary. Not on the record, that is, but we'd been together this long, and we had a three-month-old baby girl who I named after my mother, Annabelle. I wasn't in Canada, like Ava believed. I was actually an hour north of where Ava and I live, in a town outside of Richmond, Virginia.

I met Ty Peeples on a flight from Richmond to Norfolk a few years back. She was one of the flight attendants and we hit it off very well. We exchanged numbers, called one another, and things escalated from there. Fast-forward to two months later, and she invited me to her apartment, so I drove to Richmond. That night turned into a weekend-long visit and we've been together ever since. After an eight-month-long courtship, I moved Ty out of her apartment and into a home, after I found out she was having my baby. I couldn't have her raise my child in a one-bedroom apartment. My conscience wouldn't allow me.

If Ava were to find out about Ty and the baby, she'd probably try to kill me, so I would do everything in my power to keep her from finding out. Now . . . did Ty know about Ava? Of course, she did, and she's okay with it too. Did she nag me about moving in with her full-time and leaving Ava? Of course, she did. I heard it all the time. But after I reminded her about all the assets and property Ava and I have tied up together, and how it would take years and courts to divide those things up, she always backed down, and that gave me more time to live the lie that I was living.

All I had to say was: "Just give me a little more time to get up enough money to give her a settlement. That way I don't have to give all the lawyers their attorney fees in divorce court. Because, otherwise, she will bankrupt me, and then what will you have?"

It worked every time.

"Ava said someone came in and kidnapped the kids while she was asleep," I finally answered her after standing up from the bed.

"Are you serious?" She seemed baffled.

"I wouldn't joke about anything like that," I told her as I slid on my boxer briefs.

Ty sat up on the bed as if she was gathering her thoughts. "So, when did this happen?"

"She's not sure. She said that she just found the ransom note a few minutes ago. And she went to bed around midnight, so it happened after she went to sleep," I explained.

"Has she called the cops yet?"

"No."

"Why not?"

"Because the kidnappers told her not to."

"Of course, they're gonna do that, but I would call the cops anyway," she protested.

"No, I told her to wait until I get there," I said as I slipped on a T-shirt.

"Kev, I don't think that's a good idea," she pressed.

"Well, right now we're gonna do as the kidnappers want, until I say otherwise," I retorted.

The fact that Ty was pressing me about children that I had with another woman was getting underneath my skin. She needed to know that I could handle this on my own. Ava and I would handle this the way we saw fit.

"Don't you guys have a nanny?" she asked, changing her tone.

"Yes, Paulina."

"Was she there?" she probed again.

I let out a long sigh. "Yeah, she was there."

"And she didn't hear anything?" Ty questioned. She seemed suspicious of Paulina.

"She said she didn't."

"I don't know, Kev. That seems fishy to me. I mean, she could've set the whole thing up. Stuff like that happens all the time."

"No, Paulina isn't like that. She's like family. The kids look at her like their grandmother. She's been with us for years." I refuted the insinuation. My blood pressure seemed like it was climbing to an all-time high.

"Well, you can never be too sure, Kevin. People do all sorts of things for money. And she's been around for a while, so I'm sure she has an idea of what kind of money you're working with," Ty continued.

Hearing all of Ty's assumptions sent me into a fury. "Look, you don't know anything about Paulina. So shut the hell up!" I roared, and dashed out of the room.

I thought Ty was going to give me back talk, but she didn't utter a word. I was shocked, to say the least. I guess she was shocked that I would go off on her like I did. I'd never spoken to her like that before. She was probably caught off guard. To avoid any further conflict, I got dressed and immediately grabbed my things. On my way out of the house, I kissed my baby and said goodbye to Ty. I also assured her I would call her after I got home and received more information. She walked me to my car and then I left.

* * *

The drive back to Tidewater took two hours because of a traffic accident. When I finally arrived home, I felt a sense of coldness when I walked through the front door. I could instantly tell that something was wrong. There was something definitely absent, because my children always greeted me when I walked through the front door. But today that didn't happen. That, alone, felt strange. I dropped my luggage on the floor of the foyer and searched for my wife. I found her in the living room, lying on the sofa in a fetal position, face saturated with tears.

Paulina looked up and saw me standing there and announced to Ava that I was home. "Look, darling, your husband is here." But Ava was in no shape to switch her pain off and turn her focus on me.

I was flustered and consumed with so many thoughts and emotions, I couldn't tell you whether I was coming or going. Standing here in front of my wife, watching her unravel before my eyes, and trying to figure out where the fuck my kids were was becoming too much for me. Thank God for my nanny and housekeeper, Paulina. Seeing her console Ava in her motherly type of way was somewhat helping. I didn't know what we would do if we didn't have her. Paulina had been with us for about eight years now. She was like a mother to Ava and me, and a grandmother to the kids. I knew that this tragedy pained her just as much as it was hurting us.

"It's going to be all right, love. They will be returned to us safe and sound," she assured Ava as she cradled her in her arms, rocking her back and forth on the sofa.

A strong flow of tears poured from Ava's eyes uncontrollably. Her face was drenched, turning the color of her skin dark pink.

"But what if whoever has them is mistreating them?" Ava cried.

Paulina gripped Ava tighter and rubbed her back in a circular motion. "No, we're gonna think positive and believe that who-ever has them is taking good care of them. And that they will re-turn them as soon as you guys come up with the money and hand it over to them," Paulina replied.

"You heard what Kevin said—we don't have two million dol-lars!" Ava yelled out. I heard the hurt and anger in her voice. She was placing the blame on me.

"I said that I don't have it on hand," I corrected her.

Without warning she broke away from Paulina's embrace, shot up from the chair, and stormed toward me. "What the fuck is the difference? 'On hand'? Or in your possession?" she shouted.

I could tell that she wanted clarity. As badly as I wanted to tell her the truth, I couldn't. I couldn't tell her that money was tight, and what little bit I had, it was tied up in bad investments. She wouldn't understand. Hell, I wouldn't understand if the shoe was on the other foot. A year ago I was worth $15 million. Today I have a company that's only worth about $1.2 million, if I were to liquidate it. That's it. Most of that money now be-longed to one of my private investors. The home we lived in was owned by my company, and the cars we were driving were leased, so there was no money there. With the $560,000 I had in the bank, and even with the other $200,000 safely tucked away in our home safe, that still made us roughly around $1.3 million short. Now I know it's sad, but it's true.

"Look, don't worry, I'm gonna work something out," I finally said, trying to buy myself more time because I really didn't know what else to say.

"Tell me, how are you going to work it out, Kevin? I need to know what you're going to do so that we can get our kids back!" Ava roared.

This time it seemed like the whole ceiling shook. I had to admit that Ava was a firecracker. When I met her, she was a pro-fessional car thief. She worked for my best friend. They were lovers before he went to prison, and while he was there serving time, we started spending a lot of time together and fell hopelessly in love with one another. I guess she grew tired of my best friend's wild, thug lifestyle and decided she wanted a guy well respected in the community who had legitimate money coming in and wasn't rough around the edges. You know, someone she could settle down with and have a family.

Once I showed her there was more to life than stealing cars, I spent long nights on the phone with her and listened to her tell me about all of her aspirations and dreams. I realized early on that all she wanted was for someone to listen to her. Not too long after that, I found out that she liked being held at night too. And when I started cooking for her, she fell for me, hook, line, and sinker. We were deeply in love, like neither of us had ever been before.

Now it seemed that her love had shifted toward our kids. They were her world and nothing else mattered. That was why I knew it was killing her that they were gone. I just hoped that I could bring them back in one piece.

"So, are you going to answer me, or what?" she snapped. I could see the steam coming out of both ears.

"Ava, will you just give me a minute to think?" I clapped back. She was applying too much pressure on me, making me feel less than a man.

"No, fuck that! We don't have a minute. Our kids have been gone for God knows how long and you're talking about giving you a minute? You know what? Screw you! I'm calling Nick. He'll get my babies back," Ava threatened.

She whirled her body around to leave, but before she could take a step, I grabbed her by the arm. "Like hell you will," I snarled as I applied pressure. She couldn't budge.

"Let me go, Kevin," Ava shouted as she tried to loosen my grip with her free hand.

Paulina stood up and tried to reason with us from where she was standing. "Please, you guys, we should not be fighting with one another. We've got to come together and figure out a way to get our babies back. All that other mess needs to go out of the window."

Before I could give my rebuttal, my cell phone rang. I grabbed it from my pants pockets and realized that I had to take this call, so I released Ava's arm and exited the room. I heard her yelling obscenities as I headed into the garage.

"Hello," I said after answering on the third ring.

"Hey, Kev, what's up?" I heard my best friend, Nick, say.

"Man, I ain't too good right now," I said gravely.

"Tell him what's going on!" Ava shouted from the other room.

"I will," I replied, shouting loud enough so she could hear my response.

"Yo, dude, what's good?" Nick wanted to know. He seemed concerned.

I took a deep breath and sighed. "Somebody took my kids, man."

"What do you mean 'somebody took' your kids?" Nick asked. He didn't seem to understand what I was saying.

"Somebody came to my house last night while I was out of town and Ava was asleep and kidnapped my kids. They stole my fucking kids right from underneath our noses, man."

"How do you know that?"

"Because my kids aren't here and the kidnappers left a ransom note behind."

"What are they asking for?"

"They're asking for two million, Nick."

"Have you called the cops?"

"No, they warned us not to."

"How long you got?"

"To pay them?"

"Yeah."

"The note says seventy-two hours."

"Oh, shit!"

"Yeah, I know."

"You got it?"

"Nah, I don't."

"What do you mean, you *don't*?"

"Nick, I'm tapped out," I whispered. I couldn't afford to let Ava hear what I was saying.

"What do you mean you're 'tapped out'? How much do you have?"

"As far as cash?"

"Yeah."

"Close to eight hundred thousand."

"Damn, man, what happened to all of your money?"

"You know I just bought the house for Ty and the baby."

"Yeah."

"Okay, and the rest of it is tied up in the business."

"So I guess that means it's gonna be a long shot before I get a return on the money I've invested in you?"

"Come on now, Nick, you know I've been working day and night trying to secure this auto parts deal to get you your money back. And now that this has come up, I'm really fucked."

"So, what are you going to do?"

"I was hoping I could get you to help me."

"I'm sorry, but I don't have it either."

"Come on, Nick, I need you, man. My kids are gone and you're the only person I can come to with this. I have nowhere else to go."

Nick sighed. "Kev, I wish I could help you, but I'm dead in the water."

"How is that, and you got all of them motherfucking cars over there waiting to get picked up?" I instantly became enraged and shouted through the phone. I knew Nick was bullshitting me. That nigga had plenty of fucking money. I had just seen him counting over $5 million using a cash machine just the other day.

"Yo, dude, who the fuck you think you're talking to? I don't owe you a motherfucking thing, remember that!" he screamed back at me. He wasn't backing down.

"Listen, man, I'm sorry. I'm just in a bad way right now, and like I said before, you're the only person I can ask for help. I don't know anybody else I can get that kind of money from. And you know I wouldn't come to you if I really didn't need it. My children's lives are at stake. If I don't come up with this money, the kidnappers will kill them."

"You know if I had it, I would give it to you," Nick said, but again I knew he was lying to me. He was holding out on me, and I couldn't figure out why, especially in a time like this. I would do it for him in a heartbeat. My children's lives were in danger and he was acting like he didn't care.

"So you're saying you can't help me?"

"I'm just saying that I don't have the money," he replied, and then he fell silent. So I stood there with the phone in my hand, not knowing what to say next. Then he opened his mouth and spoke again. "I could probably come up with the money if you can convince Ava to do a run for me."

Hearing this come out of his mouth, and blatantly disrespect me by asking me to convince my wife to do another job for him, was mind-blowing. The job he was referring to had something to do with lifting cars. And I would die first before I let my wife get back into that game. That part of her life was over, and I refused to let her get back into it, especially at a time like this. I couldn't afford to have her out there stealing cars for her ex-lover just so we could raise the money to get our kids back from the kidnappers. Was this man out of his freaking mind?

"Absolutely not, Nick. Are you out of your freaking mind? I could never convince her to do that. Not for nothing in the world," I told him. I said it with so much anger, I wanted him to hear how appalled I was by the thought of it.

"Convince me to do what?" Ava asked. I swear, her voice came from out of nowhere.

I turned around and faced her. "I'll talk to you about it later," I said, trying to brush her off.

"No, I want to hear it now," she said adamantly. She wasn't backing off.

"I said, I'll talk to you about it later." I stood my ground.

"Are you still talking to Nick?" Ava changed the question and reached for my phone and snatched it out of my hand. I tried to grab it back from her, but she was too quick and leaped from where I was standing in the entryway of the room where we were both in.

"Nick, what is going on? What is Kevin talking about?" she abruptly asked him.

I couldn't hear what Nick was saying, but I had already had the conversation with him, so I knew what he was telling her. Then she slowly turned around and faced me, and when I saw her facial expression, it gave me a clear indication as to how she was feeling about what Nick was saying to her. Three seconds in, her facial expression began to sour.

"But, Nick, you know I'm not into that life anymore . . ." she began to say, and then she fell silent.

That's when Nick took over the conversation. I knew then that Nick was doing whatever he could to convince her otherwise.

She stood there for a few minutes and then she said, "I'm sorry, Nick, but I can't, especially right now. I mean, my children need me, and I can't jeopardize myself by putting myself in harm's way when the objective is to get them back. I mean, couldn't we work something else out? Come on now, at least for old times' sake?" she begged him.

I could tell that she was grasping for straws at this point. And Nick was making it very difficult for us. I mean, he already shut the door on me. Let's see how Ava's way panned out. When I noticed Ava shaking her head back and forth, as if she was getting annoyed, I knew that this conversation wasn't going her way. I also knew that things weren't looking good for us either. And then it happened, less than a minute later, Ava ended her call with Nick.

"So, what did he say?" I wondered aloud as she walked toward me, extending my phone in my direction.

"Nick said he doesn't have the money to lend us. But if I could do two jobs for him, he'll be able to give us the rest of the money we need to get the kids back."

"You're not gonna do it, right?"

Ava sighed heavily and handed me my cell phone. "What other choice do we have, Kev?"

"We have other choices," I told her after taking my phone back from her. I started walking out of the room. She followed me.

"And what choices are those? We have less than two and a half days to get our babies back and you don't have the slightest idea where to get the rest of the money we need!" she shouted from behind.

"I'm gonna figure it out."

"But we don't have time for that, Kevin."

I stopped in my tracks and turned to face Ava. "Sounds like you wanna do the job," I pointed out, giving her a facial gesture that I was not happy.

"If you got a better idea, then I step out of your way," was her response.

"Do you realize how stupid you sound right now?" I snapped.

"I couldn't care less how stupid I sound right now, Kevin. I'm a way maker, and at least I have a plan," she struck back.

"What if you get caught by the cops or the person you're stealing the car from blows your fucking head off your shoulders? Then what?"

"That's just a chance I'll have to take."

"Do you know how crazy that sounds? You are risking your life and freedom for some fucking money that's not even a guarantee?"